The Good Citizen

A Novel

Marc Ross

First published in 2023 by Milton Books
an imprint of Milton Books Limited
Based in the United Kingdom
www.miltonpublishing.com

ISBN: 978-1-8380665-3-6 (paperback)
ISBN: 978-1-8380665-2-9 (ebook)

For rights and permissions, contact the publisher at
books@miltonpublishing.com

Power is in tearing human minds to pieces and putting them together again in new shapes of your own choosing.

— George Orwell, *Nineteen Eighty Four*

Chapter 1

The day had started like any other cold and colorless November morning. But all that changed when the bus pulled in at the next stop.

He saw the first gunman come forward from the gloom of the alleyway between the row of houses, the second close behind, their ball caps pulled low about their eyes and their masks pulled high to their mouths as they came alongside the waiting bus like bandits on the prowl. The coal black steel of their snub-nosed revolvers cut an evil shape in the gray dawn murk.

He lowered the book he was reading and watched from the back seat through the filthy windows as the gunmen stepped on, pointing their weapons. From the patches of bare skin around their eyes, all he could tell was that one was a white boy, the other black. Both dressed in clothes ill-fitting for their rake-like frames.

The white gunman—and the bigger of the two—came

on cursing and hollering for the driver to kill the engine as he took aim with his revolver, and the wearied woman sat slanted in the front row with the nameless bulk in her belly screamed at the sight of them.

The driver raised a hand, then all eyes turned to see his head rock back on his neck. Sudden. Violent. Without mercy.

The report of the gun was short but deafening. The white gunman stood stock-still, the short barrel still leveled at the driver's forehead as the body tipped forwards against the wheel, the window behind his fresh corpse sprayed with gray matter and gore as it slid down the glass.

The gunman turned to face the passengers, his wild eyes darting back and forth between the faces of his focus. "Watch the doors," he said as his counterpart came behind him, leaving him free to work the floor.

The black gunman nodded, following orders as he put his body between the open doors of the bus.

Another holler went up somewhere.

Then another.

But not Alice.

She was silent, and yet he watched the tremble of her hand as she closed the cover of the textbook rested on her knees, and the rise and fall of her chest with every quickening breath.

He didn't know her real name. She was a stranger to him and nothing more, but she looked like an *Alice* and reminded him of a woman he perhaps used to know but could no longer place.

She sat alone, her pallid face lost amongst the weight of dark tresses that framed yet darker eyes. She wore a delicate smile and carried the look of a young woman who had yet to find her place in the world. And yet, hidden beneath her homespun manner, lied the certain glimpse of an unembellished beauty whose dark eyes yearned for something more than these simple ways.

Alice sat on the row in front of him, just like every other morning, and from where he could watch her read her textbooks before she left him at her usual stop opposite the bank on Main Street, carrying with her the faint smell of honeyed perfume.

They had never uttered a word to one another, and yet, for the past two weeks of riding the same bus, he felt like he knew her, or a part of her at least, between the morning smiles of common strangers on his way to his ordinary job in this ordinary town. A strange familiarity between the unfamiliar.

His friends called him Jack, but the name on the faded patch on his greased coveralls said *Jacob*. On any other day, he was a man of no particular proclivities. A man who wore the long, hard miles of life on an otherwise handsome face. A man as forgettable as any other in this godforsaken town.

Until today.

The white gunman moved down the gangway, past the sitting passengers with their heads turned aside, his revolver trained on the pregnant woman in the front row as he tossed an empty duffel bag beside her swollen feet. "Put whate'er you got in there."

The pregnant woman looked up at him, eyes burning, the buttons on her blouse straining about her midriff as she placed a palm over her bulging belly. "You gonna kill me too?" she said as she spat on his mask. "Sonofabitch."

The gunman held the barrel level with her eyes, unflinching, as he looked down at her belly. "Be doin' it a favor, I reckon."

She held his stare a moment longer, then emptied her pockets and placed everything she could find into the duffel bag.

The gunman pushed on up the gangway as each passenger unburdened themselves of their bodily possessions. Nobody uttered as much as a word.

Jacob could see everything from where he was sitting as the gunman drew nearer, passing the duffel bag to each passenger as he went, his partner keeping watch by the doors. He looked about the people on the bus and the paralysed expressions that hung on their faces. A grandmother two rows down turned as the gunman came forward, shielding her infant grandchild into the safety of her frail arms. And as he glanced down again, he spotted Alice's trembling thumb searching for three digits on her cellphone: 911.

He had no time to warn her, and she hadn't seen him coming.

"Everythin' in the bag!" the gunman said, pressing the barrel of the revolver hard to her temple. Alice swallowed a scream and slid her cellphone under the crook of her leg, out of sight, and emptied what she had into the duffel bag laden with the spoils of her fellow strangers.

The gunman looked down at her, eyes burning. "Cellphone?"

Alice drew in a breath, then reached a hand under her leg and handed it over.

The gunman peered down at the screen, killed the call, then raised his chin to look at her once again as he pressed the cold barrel to her cheek now. "And the necklace."

Alice pulled back and closed her eyes. "I can't give you that."

The gunman thrusted the gun into the side of her mouth. "I won't ask a second time."

She clasped the pendant in one hand and held it close to her chest. "I can't."

"What's goin' on up there?"

The gunman looked round to see his partner down the front, shifting nervously from side to side like a crack addict thirsting for a fix. "Gimme a minute!" he said.

The other gunman eyed the road nervously. Traffic building. A siren somewhere off in the distance. "We don't got a minute!"

"I said I won't ask a second time," the gunman said, turning back to Alice now.

"It's okay," said Jacob, leaning forward in his seat, sensing where this was going.

She must have felt the gentle touch of his hand on her

shoulder as she let go of a breath. Alice turned to look at him, and for the first time, he saw the person behind those dark and distant eyes.

He told her again for comfort: "It's okay."

She loosened the grip on the pendant and unclasped the chain from around her neck, tears in her eyes as she did it.

Jacob sat back in his seat as the revolver rounded on him, the gunman's hand visibly shaking, barely able to keep a steady aim. He raised both hands, one holding his cellphone, the other clutching his billfold as he placed them into the bag, then worked loose the strap on his watch.

"That all ya got?" the gunman said.

He nodded. "You picked the wrong bus in the wrong town to make it rich today, friend."

The gunman turned on him, black eyes beneath the mask. "You're no friend of mine."

"We're just regular working folk," he said, placed the watch into the bag now, his eyes dull and half-lidded, like an alligator surfacing for prey. "We got nothing but the change in our pockets. Is that worth killing for?"

"Shut your fuckin' mouth!" The gunman snatched up the bag and turned on his heel to leave, but his arm jerked backwards by the dead weight of something pulling hard against him.

Jacob looked up at him, one hand holding onto the loose strap of the duffel bag.

He saw the gunman's eyes go wide as he tried to wrest

the bag free of his callused hand, his cracked skin whitening on his knuckles as he felt the pull.

He spotted the arch of the revolver as the gunman pivoted towards him again to take aim, then released his grip on the bag as both hands went up to reach for the gun, his mind calculating a thousand details in a millisecond.

Everything else faded away as he rose to his feet and shifted his weight onto his front foot, wild eyes looking back at him as he grabbed the gunman's shooting arm with one hand, leaving his other to work the weapon itself. A round in the chamber, hammer cocked. A second later and the gunman was staring down the barrel of his own gun before he'd even noticed it had gone.

All this within the blink of an eye.

"Back up," he said as he kept the weapon trained on the gunman's chest. "Real slow."

The laden duffel bag hit the floor with a thud as the gunman lifted both hands in mock surrender.

"Now turn around." He placed the barrel of the revolver at the base of the gunman's skull as he turned from him, stroking the trigger. "You look at me again and I'll put a bullet in your brain. Understand?"

The gunman answered with a wordless nod.

"Walk."

The gunman walked forwards, a step at a time. The entire bus was silent now as they moved back down the gangway, the faces of each passenger whiter than the one before until they reached the front of the bus where the second gunman was still standing, his own weapon held in an awkward grip as he raised it.

"Your friend here made his choice," Jacob said, keeping his chest tight to the gunman's body as he addressed the kid stood before the doors. He was a kid all right. He didn't need to see the face to know the difference between a man who knew how to handle a gun and a boy whose father had never taught him how to use one. "But you've still got one. How this ends is on you."

The gunman stood hunched. "Shoot this fool, Troy!"

The kid looked hard at his friend, then down at the open doors of the bus, his hand shaking more with each passing second. Amongst the collective restraint of breaths, Jacob paused, waiting for the kid to make the next move. "What's it gonna be?" he said, the air heavy and fetid with the stench of sweat and fear.

The kid stood like some effigy awaiting his fate as his gaze shifted forward again, his head rocking from side to side as he tried to find the words. "That ain't my name." His voice was low, breaking under the weight of the moment before him.

"Troy?" he said, his tone measured, trying to level with the boy behind the mask. "Put the gun down and leave. That's all you gotta do."

The gunman stepped forward, hands flailing. "Fuckin' shoot him!"

Jacob stepped forward, matching his move, the barrel of the revolver boring a hole into the back of the gunman's head. A reminder of who was in control. "They're gonna put your friend here to sleep for what he did today," he said, looking up at the masked boy before him again. "It doesn't have to be the same for you."

Everything fell silent. Jacob held the boy's stare as he watched him inch back a step, past the dead body of the driver slumped at the wheel, towards the open doors, then turn and hightail it towards the alleyway across the street at a dead run. In another second he was gone, lost between the gray murk and the buildings from which he came.

Jacob grabbed the remaining gunman by the collar, now alone and shaking from head to limb. "Get on your knees," he said.

The gunman spat and turned to face him, his eyes more black and defiant in the dim light that found his face as the mask fell from his mouth. "You ain't gonna shoot me."

Jacob steadied his aim, finger on the trigger, yet all he could do was stare at the man in front of him who stood with crooked teeth behind a crooked smile.

The gunman came forward with a goading look in his eye. "You don't got it in ya."

He reared back as the gunman tilted his head towards the floor and dropped at the knees. Only then did he notice it: the gunman's right hand, reaching for something hidden at his leg.

The flash of a blade caught the faintest of dull light as he saw it enter his thigh. He winced as the pain shot down his leg and the revolver worked free of his grip and found the floor.

Then the gunman was facing him again, rearing like some rabid dog rid of its leash, the switchblade now bearing down once again and flecked with blood.

He raised an arm to counter the falling knife, the edge of the blade slicing open his forearm to reveal yet more blood and sinew beneath the skin. He lunged forward, forcing the gunman onto his back foot, and let swing with his right hand with wild abandon.

The gunman's head rolled back on his neck, his nose twisted and torn as fragments of bone punched through the cartilage with each unbroken blow.

Jacob staggered forward as his legs gave way from beneath him. The gunman's eyes glassed over as they went down together. Everything a blur.

The gunman hit the ground first, all the wind knocked out of him as the back of his head kissed the deck.

And then he saw it again: the heel of the blade lodged somewhere between the gunman's throat and mandible as his mouth fished open, gasping for air but finding none. Then nothing but a vacant stare looking back up at him with eyes that equally held nothing at all.

Chapter 2

Blue and red lights traveled the tops of three police cruisers parked sideways across the center-line of the highway, the bus now abandoned by the gravel berm with its doors open. Amongst it all, a crowd of dark figures stood huddled together like supplicants under a sunless sky, and beyond them yet more onlookers emerged from the murk to watch.

Jacob Keller could barely see a hand in front of his own face, and the figures that moved in the distance appeared to him like faceless specters, lost in the heavy mist that clung to the face of the buildings like a fallen veil. He couldn't see them, but he heard their blessings as they pointed and talked amongst themselves about how he had saved them from certain loss, or worse still.

He pulled his watch cap down over his cold and roughened brow as a medic saw to the gash on his forearm, packing the wound with gauze.

"Keep pressure on it," she said, wrapping tape around his arm to secure it in place. "How's your leg?"

He placed a hand on top of the gauze, the wound red-hot and biting with each turn of the wrist. "Leg's fine. Can I leave now?"

The medic glanced up at him, nonplussed. "You're going to need stitches."

"Is that necessary?"

The medic flashed a penlight in his eyes and ignored the question. "Look here," she said, moving her index finger to the left of his eyeline.

He looked left and watched a lone figure approach from the sidewalk, shoulders pulled forward, head down as she came towards him. The necklace returned to its rightful place.

"I'm not sure what to say," Alice said, lifting the collar of her faded duffle coat about her neck. She stood with her hands in her pockets, her face as ashen as the gray sky above her that was now promising nothing but rain.

"Are you okay?" he asked, noticing the falter in her voice and the awkward look in her eye, like dark stones amongst an ocean of white.

She tucked a loose fall of hair behind her ear and looked up at him again with a gentle nod. "Thanks to you."

He smiled, and she managed a smile in return. She opened her mouth to speak again, but all he heard was that of another man next to him.

"Mr. Keller?"

Jacob glanced to his right now and looked upon the enormous frame of a man in the half-light, dressed in uniform the color of faded ink, twin stars on the epaulets, the man's hands rested in the crook of his belt buckle beside his service weapon. "Yes, sir?" he said, one eye on the chief, the other still on Alice.

"Helluva thing you did," the chief said, proffering an outstretched hand. "Chief Morales." His accent was customary amongst the common stock of this blue-collar town, yet underneath it ran the lingering remains of a Mexicano drawl.

He took the chief's hand and shook it.

The chief looked down at his bandaged arm. "Don't suppose you're looking for work?"

He smiled. "Don't think I'd be much good to you right now. Besides, I never much liked paperwork."

"You and me both," the chief said, stepping back to survey the scene. "Talking of which, I'm gonna have to trouble you for a statement."

"Sure."

"We need to get him stitched up," the medic said, removing her blood-soaked gloves, a steely expression on her face. "You'll have to wait."

The chief nodded as they shared a look. Neither man was willing to bandy words with the woman. "Guess we'll speak again," he said, returning the pocketbook to the inside of his worn jacket. The chief turned and headed back towards his waiting cruiser.

Alice was gone when he looked back again. An empty spot on the sidewalk where she had been standing not a minute since. As he lifted his eyes, beyond the point where the crowd had thinned to nothing, he saw her faint silhouette as it passed the rows of vacant shops in the distance and then vanish into the white fog beyond.

———

He could smell the nurse's perfume as she leaned over him, suturing his wounds with a delicate hand.

"Think we're nearly done here," said the nurse.

"Then I can go?"

She raised her head and smiled. "Yes, then you can go."

The second thing he noticed were her painted nails, immaculate given her line of work.

"How are you feeling?"

"A sore head, but that'll be the beer last night."

"Nausea?"

Jacob shook his head, then turned it away as the nurse worked the needle on his arm. "Truth be told, I'm not too good with hospitals."

"You wouldn't be the first," the nurse said. "Sounds like you've had your fair share of them."

He regarded her with a curious expression. "You read my file?"

"It's my job to know my patients."

He looked down at the name badge pinned to her

uniform. He hadn't noticed it before, but the name etched upon it made him smile. "Joy."

She glanced up from the needle upon hearing her name. "Yes?"

"The last time I was in a hospital, I couldn't even remember my own name. But I will remember yours."

Nurse Joy smiled at the sentiment. "Can I ask what happened?"

He inhaled sharply and grimaced as she carried on stitching his wounds. "I'm not really sure."

"You still have no memory of it?"

"I was told it was a car accident."

Her expression softened at once, as if someone had died and she was left to tell the family. "Well, I guess there're times in our life when what happened before never really matters all that much."

"Maybe," he said, as he took pause at the notion. "But how can you know who you are if you can't remember where you've been?"

"All I know is I wish I could forget a few things in my life." Nurse Joy sighed and rolled her eyes as she continued her work. "Sorry. This turned real serious."

"I don't mind."

She smiled again.

It wasn't a lie, yet it wasn't the truth, either. He could remember more than he cared to admit, but the memories which remained from that day were now nothing more than faded drawings on an ever-darkening wall. Visions caught in a spectral fog. A misshapen puzzle of mismatched pieces.

He remembered leaving the plant that evening after a hard day's work. Then the flash of headlights in his rearview as he turned off for the exit ramp. But that was it.

No sound.

No pain.

Just a void in his mind.

He'd been in a coma for two weeks before he'd prized his eyes open to the waking world once again. He didn't know where he was, who he was, or why he was there. And even now, ten years gone, the memories of his life before were nothing more than aged pictures lost to time, filled with nameless faces of people he once knew, but no longer recognized. Faces that still now would come in his sleep like long departed friends to greet him, although most now gone like the days that had passed him since. But there was one that had never left his dreams. A face that both heartened and haunted him in equal measure. A face that he saw as he looked into the wide eyes of the nurse before him, hair just as red, a riot of russet and gold, and a smile as winsome to match. But he could not remember her name either.

"Mr. Keller?" said Nurse Joy.

He shook off his stupor as the nurse mumbled something again. "Sorry, what did you say?"

"Do you have family I can call? To let them know you're here?"

"No family," he said.

"Anyone else I can call for you?"

He shook his head as Nurse Joy cast a glance over his shoulder towards the door behind him.

"Excuse me for a moment." She placed the suture kit on the table beside her, got to her feet, and walked towards the door where another nurse was peering in through the glass panel. "There's water on the side if you need it."

He watched her as she slipped outside into the corridor, her voice low as she spoke to the other nurse outside, returning his stare with the occasional glance of her own.

A moment later and Nurse Joy stepped back into the room, followed by the other nurse who was all smiles and delight as she came forward to embrace him.

"I wish they made more men like you," the other nurse said, wrapping her arms around his beaten body.

He looked up at this stranger with a furrowed brow, then at Nurse Joy, who was standing at the back of the room, watching with one eye on the clock.

"Julia's sister was on the bus this morning," Nurse Joy said.

Nurse Julia stepped back again and wiped her eyes dry, struggling to get her words out. "She told me what you did for her. And my little niece or nephew, too."

Of course, he could see the likeness now. The same tired eyes as the pregnant woman in the front row. "I didn't really do much at all," he said.

"If you need a ride home... I get off in an hour." Nurse Julia let the offer hang there for a moment.

"Thank you," he said, averting his gaze. "I'll be fine."

Nurse Julia pursed her lips. "I'll be here if you change your mind."

He nodded in thanks as Nurse Joy opened the door to show Nurse Julia out.

"Looks like you might have to get used to that around here," Nurse Joy said, closing the door so it was just the two of them again.

He held her stare as she took up the chair next to him to finish stitching his wound. "How'd you mean?"

Nurse Joy lifted her head in surprise. "You haven't seen it?"

"Seen what?"

She wheeled her chair over to the counter at the far end of the room to retrieve something on top and then wheeled back again. She sat with her cellphone in her hand and scrolled through until she found what she had been looking for.

He leaned forward on the bed as she turned the phone to show him the screen.

A static image at first, then a video started to play.

Jacob watched as the scene played out, his wound half-sutured and still weeping at the edges.

On the screen, the dark figure of a body replaced the blackness, then a face. A face he knew well enough for it was his own.

He was standing with a masked figure in front of him: the gunmen, clad in black, the barrel of the revolver leveled at the back of his head as the rest of the footage played out with surprising clarity.

The blur of a switchblade as it sank into his arm.

The gunman fall to his back, eyes wide as he fought for his last breath until there was nothing left at all.

Jacob sat back again as Nurse Joy returned the phone to her pocket. "How did you get that?"

"It's all over," she said.

"All over what?"

"The news. Internet. Everyone's seen it."

"Who?"

"Who what?"

"Who put it on there?"

She shrugged. "You were on that bus. Not me."

When Nurse Joy had finished stitching him up, he stepped back out onto a white corridor filled with a sea of strange and afflicted faces, each one watching him as he started for the exit.

All eyes were on him and him alone.

Outside, the day had grown colder and bleaker still, and there was no sun nor any promise of it to come. He inhaled the icy air and let out a long breath that he watched carry forth in the slight wind that had blown in, and in the distance he saw the shape of a man leaning against a police cruiser, looking hard at him through a train of elderly and infirm bodies that separated them. The needy and the sick and the dying.

He crossed the parking lot towards Chief Morales, past a child being rushed by medics on a gurney too large for his small body, his mouth covered with an oxygen mask too large for his small face, the weeping parents close behind.

The chief finished the cigarette balanced on his bottom lip, then rubbed the stub out underneath his boot. "Mr. Keller," he said. "Need a ride?"

Chapter 3

"**Y**ou drink?" he said, holding up a can of cold Blue Ribbon.

The chief sat crossed-legged at the table, watching him with an unbroken stare that seemed to look right through you. "Not on duty," he said, closing his pocketbook rested on the table. "But I think we can call it a day."

Jacob reached into the freezer drawer, grabbed a second can, then returned to the empty chair opposite the chief, who was now admiring the spartan contents of his apartment.

"You live alone here?"

"Yes, sir."

"That figures," the chief said, getting to his feet now to study the room. "Not a bad place. Missing something, though."

"Uh huh, what's that?"

The chief noted the bare walls and empty tabletops, devoid of color and comforts. "A woman's touch."

Jacob cracked open the top of his beer and slugged it straight back. "Need a woman for that."

The chief nodded, then stood and paced the room, noting the black mold blooming in the corner of the drywall. "You should get that looked at."

"I will," he said, taking a moment to gather his thoughts. "You find the kid?"

Morales set the beer down on the table and returned to his seat. "Still looking. But we've got a good idea who he is. We have officers at his mother's trailer turning it over as we speak." Morales sipped his beer again. "I shouldn't be telling you this."

Jacob touched his forearm, wrapped in dressing. "I ain't got anyone to tell, chief."

Morales nodded. "Damn brave thing you did today," he said, rubbing the graying stubble on his chin. "Some might say stupid."

"I wasn't really thinking."

"Well, from what I've seen, you're a man who knows how to handle himself."

He turned away from Morale's pointed stare, noting his mouth curled with a trace of suspicion.

Morales reached into his breast pocket for the pack of Parliaments. "You smoke?"

"No, sir."

"Me neither," the chief said, pulling a cigarette from

the pack and lighting it. "That's what I tell the wife, anyway. Do you mind?"

Jacob slid a small jar lid across the table in which to dispense the ash. "Have you seen the footage?"

The chief nodded. "We've taken it down," he said. "But you know how it is. Once these things are out there, well, it's like a virus. No controlling it."

"I'm sorry."

The chief knocked back the rest of his beer, smoked his cigarette, then got to his feet again. "You leave that for us to worry about."

"What happens next?" he said, as he stood to join him.

"You going anywhere I need to know about?"

"No, sir."

"Good. Keep your head down if you can," the chief said, handing him his card. "I don't wanna see you in the news or in the papers, either."

Jacob nodded, pocketing the card as he walked the chief to the door. "No, sir."

Morales threw on his jacket and pulled his ball cap low to his eyes. "Thanks for the beer."

A burst of camera flash lit up the street as the chief opened the door, like fireflies scattering in the forest, the faces behind them unseen through the bright white strobes as a swarm of photographers descended upon the sidewalk.

Jacob took shelter behind the door, out of sight.

The chief turned to leave, holding up a hand to shield

his eyes to see his cruiser parked beyond the glow of lights at the side of the road.

Jacob closed the door on the world and pulled the shades, then wandered back into the silence of his apartment. He swallowed down the rest of his beer, tossed the empty can to one side, got another from the refrigerator, then placed another can from the freezer drawer in its place. He looked across his stark walls towards the bookcase at the far end, the only thing in the way of furnishings save for the threadbare couch that was fraying at the seams, and the small television set atop the cheap melamine unit.

Paperback novels lined the bookshelf. Just the classics: Aligheri, Byron, Camus, Dumas, Faulkner, Hardy, and Huxley. On the shelf below were Joyce and Kafka and Lovecraft and Melville and McCarthy. And below that the works of Orwell and Proust and Shelley and Steinbeck and Tolstoy and Vonnegut. There were countless more, each book tattered and worn at the edges, just like books were supposed to be.

He let his eyes drift from shelf to shelf, a small gap between Hardy's *Jude the Obscure* which tilted sideways towards Huxley's *Brave New World*. The gap which was missing his most treasured book of all. The only one that he carried with him everywhere he went: Melville's *Moby Dick*, nowhere to be seen.

He must have left it on the bus because he had been reading it that very morning, right before the gunmen had come on brandishing their weapons.

He could almost see it now, the spine broken in two on the back seat.

————

Outside, the light was failing fast, and the stars were up in their masses, burning like white-gold embers against a curtain of black. He stood at the rear window and watched the last of the dismal sun pass from sight, behind the broken hills to the west and below the tops of the rundown houses.

Above him, he could hear the swell of lovemaking, but not of the tender kind. This was rough, angry sex, like a jackhammer threatening to work its way through the ceiling.

He drank his beer and checked the clock on the wall as he turned on the radio to drown out the carnal moans from the woman that lived above. It was her 8pm call, and like clockwork, her trade started at sundown.

He cranked the radio dial all the way until he could hear nothing but Roots rock and the sound of the Heartland. Skynyrd and Mellencamp and Springsteen. He'd listen all night if he had to.

————

He had a glass of Coke ready for when the boy arrived, his small face staring back at him through the patio doors whilst his aunt upstairs got down to business.

"It's cold out there tonight," he said, unlocking the door and stepping to one side to let the boy into the warm.

The boy came in and went straight for the glass of Coke. "Saw you on the TV today."

"That so?"

"Mm-hmm." The boy sipped the Coke and wiped his mouth, his fingers black with dirt. "Said you killed a man."

Jacob furrowed a brow. "I didn't kill nobody."

The boy rolled his eyes. "I'm not stupid."

He took another swig of beer, not wishing to discuss the matter further, especially with a ten-year-old.

"I think what you did was real cool," the boy said.

"No, it wasn't," he said. "And don't you go taking lessons from me."

"If you say so."

He looked down at the boy and studied the blue welt above his left eye, just below his matted and filthy hair. "I do say so."

"Mm-hmm."

"Where've you been?"

The boy lifted his head as he stood, his clothes too big for his scraggy frame. "Been nowhere."

"You sure about that?"

The boy feigned a nod.

"Then tell me how you got that bruise?"

The boy turned and said nothing.

"Ben?" he said, squatting to his level now. "Tell me, who did that to you?"

The boy was still, silent.

"I'll keep asking until you tell me."

"Kid at school," the boy said.

"Does your aunt know about this?"

The boy shook his head now. "I told nobody but you."

"You skipping school?"

"No."

"Don't be lying to me."

"Okay. A couple of times."

"Where'd you go?"

"Nowhere."

"Ain't no such place."

The boy sighed. "Sometimes I go to the old rail yard. It's quiet there."

"You've got no place being there on your own. It's dangerous." He got to his feet again. Ben was a good kid. The quiet kind. But the boy had seen more terrible things in his ten years than most men ever would by the time they were gray and old and ready to die. He had enough to deal with at home with a crackhead for an aunt who'd rather spend her time riding old men for a measly buck than teaching the boy the ways of the world so he could avoid the same mistakes that she made. The boy had never spoken of his mother, but there was nothing good to come from that story anyway, of that he was certain.

They both looked at each other as the moans from upstairs suddenly dwindled to nothing.

"Have you eaten?" he said.

The boy shook his head and set the empty glass down on the counter.

The fridge was bare when he looked in again. A half-eaten cheesesteak hoagie on a plate and some apple slices in a tupperware box that were browning at the edges. He opened the cupboard, spotted a pack of elbow macaroni on the otherwise empty shelf. "You like pasta?"

The boy looked up with an eager nod, his mouth creased and watering.

"Good," he said. "You lay the table."

The boy jumped to his feet and gathered the glassware and two plates from the cupboard and set them down on the small table in the corner. When he came back, the boy stood and watched as Jacob boiled a pan of salted water on the stovetop. He had that look in his eye that held a burning question. That same desperate look he'd seen more times than he'd cared to admit. Mouth turned down on one side. A dry swallow in his throat. Hands shuffling together.

"I know what you're gonna ask and the answer is yes," he said, wishing to put the boy out of the misery of asking. "You can sleep on the couch tonight."

The boy's eyes lit up, and a smile crept across his face.

Jacob swilled down the last of his can and tossed the empty to one side. "Now go grab me another beer so we can eat."

Chapter 4

Marcus Quinn sat back in his chair and studied the inmate opposite him: a rake of a man, his face a sallow and drawn sag of bloodless skin, as though he'd been deprived of light for a hundred years and counting.

The inmate returned the stare and rested his manacled hands flat against the table in front, his nails filthy and yellow at the tips.

They were sitting in a colorless and airless room with nothing but a one-way mirror, a table, two chairs, and a panic alarm mounted to the wall. To Quinn's left sat another man, dressed in a wool sweater and matching brown tie. He'd guessed he was no older than thirty-five, although he'd never cared to ask.

"I'm Dr. Fraser," said the man next to him, pushing his glasses back on the bridge of his nose.

The inmate rapped his fingers on the desk, deadpan,

as though he had some other place to be. "And who is this?"

"This is my colleague, Mr. Quinn," Fraser said.

Quinn just sat there and observed, just like they paid him to do. Nothing more. Nothing less.

"I'm intrigued to know what you have to speak to me about that couldn't be said on a phone call," the inmate said, pursing his lips now. He was erudite and spoke with a lisp. On the surface, he held the appearance of college-stock. An educated man.

"Mr. Garett," Fraser said, leaning forward in his chair now as he addressed the inmate. "We've shortlisted you as a candidate for a new program. We wanted to speak to you in person and discuss your potential involvement in that."

There was a flicker of interest on the inmate's face now that had not gone unnoticed. Quinn folded his arms as Eugene Garett, three-times convicted baby killer, yawned a feigned indifference.

"This all sounds very exciting for you," Garett said, taking pause for a moment. "But I'm struggling to see what benefit this has to my situation."

Fraser adjusted his tie and sat forward. "If you were interested in helping us, I assure you it would be a reciprocal arrangement."

"Perhaps you could be more specific?"

"Reduced jail time." Quinn said, watching for Garett's reaction.

Fraser cleared his throat. "Yes, that's one option at our discretion."

Garett sighed and tucked a wisp of gray hair behind his ear as he considered it for a long moment. "What is it you're asking of me, exactly?"

"Your participation." Fraser said, pushing his glasses back on his face again with a forefinger. "We can't discuss specifics at this stage."

The inmate lifted his head as his eyes scanned the room for his next thought. "You want me to take you on your word, is that right?"

Fraser nodded. "This is a onetime offer. There are many others who would long for this opportunity."

Garett curled his lip into some ungainly smile. "And what is the nature of your profession, might I ask?"

"Forensic psychology," Fraser said.

"Which college?"

"Stanford."

Garett lifted a brow in acknowledgement, then pointed to Quinn, but kept his focus on Fraser as though there were only two men in the room. "And him?"

Quinn could feel Fraser looking at him, waiting for him to answer for himself. But he kept his gaze fixed upon the pale inmate on the opposite side of the table.

"Mr. Quinn is not a medical colleague," Fraser said.

"What does that mean?"

"It means he's here to observe."

Garett smiled a crooked smile. "And does Mr. Quinn speak for himself, or is that your job, too?"

The room fell silent as Fraser shifted awkwardly in his seat.

Quinn looked on as Garett grinned in his direction. "You can sit and rot in your shithole cell for the rest of your days for all I care," he said, leaning forward across the table, eye to eye with the gutless freak. "Or you can do something worthwhile with what's left of your miserable life."

Garett considered it for a moment. "You certainly have a way with words. A police officer, I assume. Am I right?"

Another silence followed.

"Mr. Quinn's occupation is not important," Fraser said, trying hard to steer the conversation back to the issue at hand.

"Yes, I know that look." Garett sniffed the air and pulled some wretched face. "The smell too."

"Not anymore," Quinn said, and the words came out through gritted teeth.

Garett raised another shit-eating smile, the nerve he'd struck all too apparent.

Fraser leaned across the table and whispered into his ear. "Perhaps leave this one to me."

Garett watched on with mild amusement, then Quinn stood and arched his back and started for the door, a slight limp as he went.

He could hear Garett sniff the air again as he closed the door behind him and stepped out into a corridor of the jail. He let out a breath, then followed the corridor to the adjoining observation room, where he continued watching from behind the one-way mirror. The walls were black and padded with sound proof panels to prevent any sound leakage, and there was a microphone which fed back to a mini-speaker mounted to side of the observation panel from which he could hear every spoken word.

It was the first time in as long as he could remember that he'd had to exercise some restraint. He wanted to hurt that bastard more than he liked to admit, which is exactly why he was perfect for work that was strictly off-the-books.

As he stood by the one-way mirror, looking in at Garett—who was now appearing to enjoy the undivided attention—he heard Fraser's voice come through the speaker.

"Could you tell me about the circumstances leading to your incarceration here at Fayette?" Fraser said, his voice soft and reposeful again, yet tinny through the speaker.

"Dr. Fraser," Garett said with a shake of the head. "Please, let's not waste each other's time here with fatuous queries. You and I both know you already know my history. Why else would you be here?"

"I'd like to hear it from you."

Garett sighed and sat forward, picking at his finger-nails. "You want to hear about all those boys I've killed? How I washed their bodies and put makeup on them so I could imagine them as my private doll collection?"

"Is that what happened?"

"Of course." Garett laughed now. "I'm the only guilty man in this place, it seems."

Quinn recoiled at the thought and watched through the tinted window.

"One of those boys had eyes much like yours," said Garett, leaning forward across the table, licking the broken skin about his bottom lip as he watched Fraser. "Same mouth too. Plump. Ready. Yes, he looked a lot like you."

Fraser swallowed dry and shifted in his seat, one eye on the door.

At once, Garett sat back again, his withered arms folded together, owning this moment. "But now's not the time to discuss specifics. Am I right?"

Fraser closed his notepad and got to his feet. "Perhaps you'll give some thought to what I've said today."

"Oh, I will," Garett replied, smiling now. "I'll have my people contact yours."

———

They quit the main entrance of the penitentiary, past the corrections officer standing guard on the gatehouse, who waved them out.

"I like him," Fraser said, wiping the sweat from his brow with a handkerchief.

Quinn drove with one hand on the wheel as the other scrolled through his phone.

"Quinn?"

He looked up, barely acknowledged the question. "The man's a walking disease. I've always been of the opinion that there should be a special place reserved for people like him." He slowed the car as he checked his phone again.

"What is it?" Fraser said, craning his neck to look at the phone.

"It's from the director."

"Go on."

Quinn handed him the phone as he hit the replay button on the screen, then carried on driving.

"What am I looking at here?"

"Two crackheads hold up a commuter bus. One gets away. The other ends up with a switchblade through his throat."

Fraser pulled a face. "So what?"

"Keep watching."

A moment later and Fraser lifted his head again, his face now expressionless as he studied the freeze frame of the last image on the screen.

"Jacob Keller," Quinn said.

Fraser could barely bring himself to look up from the image of Keller's face. "When was this?"

"Yesterday."

Fraser rubbed his face. "Is this going to be a problem?"

Quinn eyed the road ahead, nothing but wide open country. "I was hoping you'd tell me."

Chapter 5

He woke in a tangle of damp bedsheets, a film of sweat across his chest, his body burning.

It was the dream that had stirred him. It always was. The nameless woman that plundered his dormant mind in the dead of night, calling his name as though it were a curse. The devil's hour had passed, but daylight was still truant.

Jacob's eyes eased open to the waking world and a room as dark as a fathomless well. His mind was present, but his body was not his own. He knew he was awake from the shafts of light that cast strange shadows across the walls, yet his limbs were numb and unmoving, as though stuck in some frozen husk. A motionless mute trapped in a conscious carcass. The paralysis always passed, but he counted the seconds until he could feel his body again.

Ten seconds.

Twenty seconds.

The sensation returned to his toes first, like small

needle pricks on the surface of the skin. Then a creeping sensation up his legs. A prickle down the spine. Pin jabs in his fingers, then, finally, the rest of him.

He sat up in his bed, his body still beading a cold sweat like a lingering fever. The dream of the nameless woman had not been an unhappy one, at least to start with. A foggy trail of a memory more than a dream, and yet not quite that either.

His body ached when he moved, a tenderness in his leg and a sting in his arm from the wounds. He had dreamed of the woman smiling as they walked together across a high bluff, looking out to an endless salt chuck so strong he could almost smell it in his hair. But as quick as that image had come to him, another took its place, as though time had dissolved and taken with it that contented moment between them. This time he was watching her—the same woman—lying on the floor of some unknown room, her body twisted into some unhuman shape, arms splayed by her side, a bone sticking out of her neck as her lifeless eyes sat in pools of burst blood vessels that had turned the white parts a weeping crimson. There was no sense of time nor place, just the fragmented images of this nameless woman of whom he knew nothing at all.

The only familiar thing to every dream was that it always ended the same way. The woman's dead countenance engrained into the very fabric of his mind.

When he could move his body again, he sat on the end of his bed and took in a long breath as a hand searched absentmindedly for something in the top drawer of the nightstand. He pulled out a small, clear pot, popped open the lid, and tipped a yellow pill into his hand. He swallowed it back with a glass of water as though it were some kind of morning ritual, then stood to stretch and went to the shower.

———

The hot water was like blistering barbs on his back, but it reminded him he was alive after all. After he'd washed off the grim remnants of the night before, he wrapped his arm in fresh dressing, then got dressed and made the bed. He opened the drapes and looked out at the first light of day that was just visible in the infant sky to the west.

The boy was up and waiting for him when he came out, his eyes ringed with dark and sleepless circles, much like his own.

"You're late," the boy said.

"Late for what?"

Ben poured out two bowls of raisin oats and handed him a spoon. "For work."

He made for the refrigerator and checked his rota tacked to the side. "Shit."

"Sure they won't mind," said the boy, "after what happened yesterday and all."

"I missed yesterday, too."

Ben filled his mouth with milky oats and shrugged.

He came beside the boy perched on the end of the

stool and filled a clean mug with hot coffee fresh from the pot.

"You read all those?" the boy asked, his gaze turned towards the bookshelf at the far end of the room, counting the endless spines of books lined up end to end.

"All of them."

The boy got to his feet and walked over to the wall of books and picked out one from the middle shelf. "What's this one about?" he said, turning the novel over in his palm to read the back of the dust jacket of Golding's *The Lord of the Flies*.

"It's about a bunch of boys... about your age, I'd guess," he said, rising to join him now.

"What happens?"

"They get stranded on an island alone together."

The boy looked up at him, brow raised in interest. "No adults?"

"Nope."

"Then what?"

"Why don't you read it and let me know."

Ben peered down at the book again and leafed through the pages, undisturbed by the sudden noise of the doorbell.

Jacob placed his bowl of cereal down on the countertop and started for the door. "Good morning," he said as he opened it onto a familiar face.

She looked worse than usual, her skin visibly mottled beneath the patches of streaked concealer two shades darker than her natural pallor. "Is he here?" the woman asked, her arms covered with old sores and new ones alike.

He nodded and called for the boy. "Ben, it's your aunt." Behind her, he spotted the line of media vans parked on the side of the otherwise empty street.

A moment later, the boy appeared beside him, looking up at his aunt with a mouthful of cereal as though he hadn't eaten in days.

"You okay?" the woman said, a slur in her speech from all the shit running through her veins. The haggard look of a woman who'd been up all night from too much coke and coitus.

"I'm okay," the boy said, eyes on the floor now as if searching for his shoes.

"I didn't know you left your room last night..."

The boy stood without another word to say for himself.

"Come on now," she said. "You've got school."

The boy stepped out to meet his aunt; the book pressed hard to his chest beneath his folded arms.

"Thank you," the woman said, looking up at him as she placed a hand on her nephew's head. "Again."

"No need to keep thanking me," he said, then turned to face the boy again. "Let me know how you get on with the book."

Ben lifted a hand in his departing as his aunt followed behind him. "I will."

———

He finished the rest of his coffee before it got cold and not five minutes had passed when he heard Gabe Jenkins' Jeep Cherokee pull outside his apartment, horn blaring.

Gabe was sat hunched behind the wheel of the idling truck as Jacob stepped out onto the sidewalk, his own rusted Ford Bronco left abandoned on a small patch of dirt beside the apartment block.

He did his damnedest to sidestep the reporters who descended on him like parasites thirsting for blood. He kept his head low, chin to his chest as he walked straight for the Cherokee and jumped in the passenger side, the chief's friendly warning fresh in his mind from the night before.

"I'll be damned," Gabe said, looking out at a sweep of faces jostling for position at the window as bursts of camera flash caught his wide smile. "It's a goddamned freak show out there."

"Just drive," he said, pulling his ball cap low to shield his face.

"You're a certified name in these parts now. This is your fifteen minutes. Enjoy it, Jack."

"I don't care for it, and I don't much care for talking about it, either."

Gabe shot him a look, taken aback by the curt and laconic reply. "Jesus. Okay. We don't gotta talk if that's how it is."

"That's how it is."

Gabe rolled his eye, then pointed to the Ford Bronco

beyond the swarm of photographers. "Still ain't got your truck fixed, I see."

"You know I ain't. Where're you going with this?"

Gabe shifted the Cherokee into drive. "Just a friendly reminder who's doing who a favor here, big wheel."

"Ain't a favor when I'm paying you."

Gabe smiled to himself as he steered the truck through the line of reporters foaming at the mouth. "Well, I can always drop you off at the next bus stop if you'd prefer? See how that works out for you?"

Jacob sighed and turned his head from the camera flashes as they went. "I hope God gave you a big dick, Gabe, 'cause he sure as hell shortchanged you on brains."

"Rather dick than brains, Jack," Gabe said, pulling away at speed now. "Maybe that's where you've been going wrong all this time."

———

Jacob slotted his card into the punch clock on the wall as he entered the locker room and was met with handclaps and backslapping from the twelve men stood at their lockers getting changed into their grease-stained coveralls.

One man laughed as he came forward. He never thought to ask him his real name, but the others called him *Mouth*, owing to how much he liked the sound of his voice.

"Look who it is," Mouth said, between the slow claps

of hands and whistling. "*Mr. New Brunswick*. In the flesh. Putting us on the map."

Jacob ignored the regular sallies and wisecracks as he opened his locker and emptied the contents of his pockets inside. Cellphone and billfold.

"C'mon, Jack, tell all," said another man, stood bare-chested as he changed into his work clothes, the name *Stan* embroidered onto the patch on his breast pocket.

"Can't talk about it," he said, trying to avoid all eye contact.

Stan laughed to himself. "It's all over the interweb. Everyone's talkin' about it but you."

Jacob put on a clean set of coveralls without turning. "Well, then you know what happened already."

"Big wheel's a little shaken up about it. Ain't that right?" Gabe said, stepping in to save him from the awkward silence that had now settled over the locker room.

"I'm just fine," he replied.

"C'mon, Jack. We're all friends here," Mouth said. "I can't tell if you're just being humble or you think you're better than us now."

"Neither. I just don't want to talk about it, that's all." As he went to leave, he felt a wrench on his arm as Gabe pulled him to one side.

"Listen, I've worked with these guys long enough to know they can be assholes from time to time," Gabe said, keeping his voice low enough so no one else could hear.

"But you've gotta try to fit in here because you're starting to make me look bad."

"How's this anything to do with you?"

"You seem to forget who put you up for this job."

"Well, you're always quick to remind me."

Gabe eyeballed him. "I'm just trying to help you here. You understand?"

He nodded. "Sorry."

Gabe sighed and looked about the empty room where all the other men had left for their stations. "Let's get to work."

He could barely hear himself think over the din of bestial machines. The hammer of drill-presses gave way to the whirring of belt-wheels and lathes, but amongst all the crushing of gears and metal-stampers, he found his peace as his calloused hands worked the punch-press, every movement on the hand wheel acting like some unconscious command from within.

Like all the others before him, he was a man absorbed in his work, lost to the menacing speed and synchronicity of it all. And all around him, more labored hands worked their respective machines, estranged from one another, dulled by the repetitive and deafening nature of their work.

It was only when he looked up again that he noticed the foreman stood at the other end of the punch-press, watching him through his safety glasses and clutching a clipboard in all his vainglory.

He paused and wiped the sweat from his brow and

looked at Stan, who was working the second punch-press next to him, his hands moving twice as fast as his own, like some unwearied machine that knew no end.

The foreman scribbled a note on his clipboard, then moved off, back up the shop floor, towards the mezzanine offices upstairs.

———

They paused for lunch when the claxon sounded at noon, and everyone downed their tools and killed their machines and headed like wordless mutes for the canteen.

"Jack?" the voice came from behind him as he removed his earplugs. Behind him stood the foreman again, a solemn look upon his face. "Can we have a quick word upstairs?"

"Upstairs?"

The foreman nodded, waiting for the other workers to move off, but they all turned to see, noticing one of their own missing from the rank. "It'll just take a few minutes."

Jacob wiped the grease from his hands on the back of his coveralls and followed the foreman up the stairs towards the supervisor's office, watched closely by the eyes of the other men from the shop floor below.

Bill Horton, the supervisor of this concern, glanced up from behind his desk as he entered. "How're you doing, Jack?" The foreman ushered him in and closed the door behind him.

"I guess that depends on the reason you called me in here."

Horton removed his spectacles and laid them down on the desk in front, the temple tips chewed down to the metal. "Take a seat."

"I'll stand, if it's all the same to you, sir." Behind him, he felt the looming presence of the foreman stood slightly to his side.

Horton nodded. "I heard about the incident yesterday. Wanted to check in to see how you're doing?"

"I'm fine." he said, rolling the sleeve down on his bandaged arm.

Horton sat in silence, gathering his next thoughts.

"What's this about, Bill?"

Horton cleared his throat. "I like to think all the men and women here at Horton Precision are one of my own." He leaned back in his leather chair to admire the framed picture of his family on the wall. "That's why I try to help out where I can. All the men downstairs know that about me."

"Yes, sir."

Another silence followed as Horton drew in a long breath. "You're a good man, Jack, so I'm going to get right to it," he said, sitting forward again and folding his arms across his chest. "You're just not where we need you to be."

He checked his shoulder and saw the foreman looking back at him with a smug look on his face. "You're letting me go?"

Horton rubbed his hands together as though in discomfort. "I'm not a fan of that turn of phrase."

"It's okay," he said, and that much was true. He knew this day had been coming for a while.

Horton pursed his lips and stood. "I'll get your paycheck ready before you leave, but if there's anything else I can do…"

"Know anyone who's hiring?"

Horton smiled. "I hear the school is looking for drivers. My wife is friends with the principal there. She's tough, but I don't mind putting in a good word."

"Thank you."

Horton came round to the front of his desk with an outstretched hand. "I'm sorry it's got to be this way."

"Me too," he said, taking the man's hand in his, then closing the door again on his way out.

————

He cleared out his locker, then turned to see Gabe stood at the far end of the locker room, leaning against the door frame and chowing down the rest of his sandwich.

"He's letting you go, isn't he?" Gabe said, coming forward to meet him now.

"Looks that way," he replied, closing his locker door for the last time. He grabbed his work bag off the floor and started for the double doors to the exit, past the punch clock without a second look.

"Wait a minute," Gabe said, tossing the rest of his

sandwich into the trash as he followed after him. "I'll talk to Bill. Ask him to reconsider."

He stopped and turned and placed a hand on his Gabe's shoulder. "No need. I'll talk to you later."

"Jack? Just give me a minute…"

But he was already gone, through the main gates as he crossed the parking lot towards the empty sidewalk on the main drag into town, past the rows of shuttered shops and vacant units that now dotted this once fine, blue-collar town. A town that now lied in the stone-broke shadow of its prosperous youth. New Brunswick once belonged to old money, but old money had long lost its worth in these parts. All that remained now was the picture postcard of paint-peeled houses with beat-up trucks on the drive, and the decaying edifice of the town's blast furnace that just about kept the heart of this rust belt community from flatlining completely. New Brunswick was the place he called home, and home was where the heart dwelled for unventured souls like himself.

The walk to town was only a mile, but he kept his head low as he went, bracing against the westerly wind that had blown in from the night before and showed no shows of relief.

He had a dozen missed calls from numbers unknown to him and messages from journalists promising him the world for a few words. He scrolled through the list and landed on another message from a name that he did recognize.

He made a note of it for later, pocketed his cellphone and carried on walking the rest of the way into town. His next stop was the First Commonwealth Bank on Main Street.

Chapter 6

He stepped in out of the cold wind and rain and shook down his coat, and held the door open for an old couple on their way out quarreling about their lack of wherewithal. Jacob withdrew the manilla envelope from his coat pocket and approached the pretty clerk at the cash window, busy transferring notes from one register to another. He didn't recognize her at first. It was the way her hair hanged loose about her shoulders that was different, her dark tresses usually tied up with a barrette. But when she looked up at him, there was a warmth behind the exchange of a knowing glance.

"Hi," said Alice, as beautiful as ever.

He smiled at her, then spotted her real name on the badge pinned to her blouse. "Amanda..." he said.

She looked at him awkwardly. "That's me."

He raised his head to look at her again, unaware he had said it aloud. "How are you?"

"I'm fine," she said. "And you?"

"I'm good."

She let her head fall gently into a nod as her eyes fell away from his. "Can I help you with something?"

He slid one end of the envelope underneath the small gap in the security glass. "I need to deposit this into my account."

"Sure," she said, removing the crisp handwritten check from inside. "Do you have your bank card?"

He presented his card as she looked over the check.

Amanda typed something into the computer, then placed the check into a machine that swallowed it. "For something nice?"

"It's my severance pay."

She looked up at him again, red-faced as the moment passed. "I'm sorry."

"Don't be. I didn't like the job much anyway," he said, clearing his throat. "But I'll be spending it on the only woman in my life."

"Uh huh?" Amanda said, a flash of disappointment behind the intrigue.

"My truck's been on the fritz for a good month now, so I need to get her repaired."

Amanda smiled again. "Does that mean I won't be seeing you on the bus anymore?"

"Guess so."

Her eyes fell from his again as her hands worked the keys on the computer. "Okay, that's all done," she said, presenting him with the deposit slip in the pass-through tray.

"Thank you." He looked at her and she looked back at him as another awkward silence followed. He rubbed his chin, then turned on his heel to go, but before he got to the door, he heard her voice again.

"Wait..." she said, calling out across the bank floor as she came to join him. "My father owns a repair shop just outside town. He'd be happy to look over your truck."

He stood wordlessly for a moment. "That's a very kind offer—"

"It's not kindness," she said, noticing his reticence. "And I can tell you're not the type to accept charity. So, consider it a favor from me."

He nodded politely and drew in a breath. "You have the address?"

She scribbled a note on a blank slip of paper and passed it to him. "It's on Tacoma Road."

"I know the place."

"And that's my number on the back. In case you need to, you know... can't get hold of him right away."

"Thank you," he said, taking the slip of paper as he turned to go again. "My name's Jacob, by the way. But everyone calls me Jack."

She beamed at him with the nicest smile he had seen in the longest time. "Nice to meet you, Jacob."

"You too."

———

He walked the rest of the way home in the rain, but there was nothing on his mind but the beautiful woman whose real name he could finally hold dear.

Through the wet and barren streets, he arrived at his apartment, the media vans lined up along the curb like some pestilent swarm lying dormant to greet him. He took the back entrance to avoid them and scaled the dying hedgerow that had long seen better years. When he picked himself up out of the wet dirt and dusted himself down, he glanced up and spotted the rear door to his apartment slightly ajar and swinging on its hinges in the high wind, and the silhouette of a figure moving inside.

He reached for an old grub axe discarded amongst the remnants of wet lumber that dotted the rear yard; the haft made of rotting hickory as he held the wet stock in his palm. He listened but could hear nothing, all sound lost to the gathering clouds and squall. He didn't call out. He'd take no chances. There were men out there with the means and the motives to hurt him for his small deed that had caught the attention of many. After all, the boys who had stepped onto that bus that day were sons to some poor mothers too, and one of them was now dead, his body lying somewhere dark on a cold table for his sins.

He looked up again as a shadow passed between the window inside. As he slid open the door and stepped in, he felt the soles of his boots slip on the cheap linoleum. He carried on, through the kitchen and into the living room, the axe hanging at his side and the place as quiet as he left it that morning. When he got halfway down the hallway towards the bedroom, he heard the flush of the toilet from the bathroom. He felt his body go rigid as the door opened and his grip tighten on the haft of the grub axe.

A second later and the thin frame of the boy stepped out of the bathroom, rawboned and hollow-cheeked as he tightened his belt buckle with one hand and held *The Lord of the Flies* with the other. They locked eyes with one another, and the boy staggered back at the sight of the axe above his head. "Jesus Christ. What are you doing here, Ben?"

The boy took a second or two to gather himself. "My aunt's out."

"How did you get in?"

The boy pulled out a key from his pocket. "You keep a spare under the rock."

Jacob laughed to himself as he lowered the axe again and set it down. "Nothing gets past you, huh?"

"Sorry."

"Nevermind. I thought you were someone breaking in."

The boy followed him back into the kitchen and placed the book down on the table. "I finished it," he said.

"Already?"

Ben nodded with a glum expression. "Poor Simon."

He raised a brow and smiled. "Yeah, poor Simon," he said. "What did you think?"

"I think the world is full of savages."

It wasn't what the boy said that took him aback, but the way he said it, like some revelation out of the darkest corners of the human condition and known only to those who dared to question its truth. "You might be right. Sometimes I wonder how we made it this far."

"They weren't nice kids."

"Well, I guess no one knows who they really are until they have to fight to remain alive."

"What about adults?"

"What about them?"

"Are they savages too?"

"Sure they are. Sometimes they're worse."

"How come?"

"Adults should know better. We have laws that tell us that, but we still kill each other, anyway."

The boy considered it for a long while as he approached the bookshelf. "You have anything else I can read?"

He joined the boy and picked out another book from the bottom shelf. "Try this one," he said, handing him his tattered copy of Orwell's *Animal Farm.* As he left the boy to read, he got a cold beer from the freezer drawer.

"Why do you drink that?" the boy said.

Jacob cracked open the can and swilled down a mouthful. "One day, you'll learn that every man comes to rely on something that makes his days more bearable."

"Can I try it?"

"I don't know. Have you got hair under your arms yet?"

The boy reached a hand to his armpit and shook his head.

"Then hell no, you can't."

As the boy found a spot by the window to read the book, the moment of stillness was stolen by the banging of bedposts above their heads and the carnal howls of a woman in her climax.

They shared an awkward glance. Then the boy reached for the radio to turn it up, loud enough to drown out his embarrassment at the sound of his aunt in congress.

Jacob stood and walked over to the sidetable. "You know how to play five-card draw?" he said, pulling out a deck of cards.

The boy shook his head.

"C'mon, I'll show you."

Chapter 7

He dreamed of the woman again that night. The one whose face he feared each night as his eyes tired and grew heavy. The woman that existed between the realms of some parallel life conjured up by his own wildest fancy. She terrified him in the way she sat watching him from the rocking chair in the corner of the room as he looked on from the comfort of the bed. And yet, in the same breath, consoled him in the way she drew her smile as she cradled the unseen infant in her arms. She hushed him as he went to speak, then glanced down at the child latched to her breast, the soft angles of her countenance visible in the slow shifting shafts of blue light breaking through the drapes. She looked perfect. He sat and said nothing and just watched the nameless woman as she fed the child in the dark corner.

Was it her child? His child? Perhaps theirs together?

He watched her smile scatter as a tear fell down her cheek and the child, too, began to whimper now. He went to speak again but could not open his mouth to find the words, his lips sealed shut like some silenced heathen. All he could do was watch from the warmth of the bed as the child's whimpers swelled to wailing cries and the woman's tears turned to blood as they ran down the hollow folds of skin that lined her mouth. He could not speak or move at all, his recumbent body frozen as though someone or something had sucked every sinew from his being and left him but a limp carcass. All he could do was watch as the infant's small but piercing yells grew louder still and the woman sat unmoving, her tears of blood now trickling onto her breast and atop the infant's hairless head as her own suffering cries finally tore him from his slumber.

———————

Jacob woke in the dark of his apartment, slumped forward on the sofa, ripped from the depths of his dream as though some violent force of nature had taken hold of him. An empty bottle of beer was rested on his lap as he wiped away the spittle that had collected at the side of his mouth, more empty bottles strewn about the cheap coffee table propped up by small chocks of timber cut to size to keep it steady. It was dark, and the clock on the wall turned another minute. 8:23 p.m.

He breathed hard, his lungs trying to stretch through the tightness of his chest. The wretched hollers from his dream replaced by the shrill knell of the doorbell. He got to his feet, unable to place himself for a moment. His body was present, yet his mind was still lost to whatever dark hell it had woken from. He collected up the empty beer bottles in a hurried stupor and tossed them into the trash as the doorbell rang again. It was only then that he noticed the boy had gone. Then he remembered he had sent him home in the night when the noise had stopped upstairs.

The face which greeted him on the other side of the door was a familiar one, and she stood there in her black suit and blouse like she had come straight from her office in the heart of the Steel City.

"Dr. Moss?" he said, surprised to see the woman on his doorstep.

"Hello, Jacob," said Moss, glancing back over her shoulder to count the number of reporters that had now exited their vans in their haste. "Can I come in?"

He stepped aside and Moss closed the door behind her as the reporters swarmed the sidewalk.

Erin Moss was a woman of particular poise. She stood with a back as straight as a pillar and clutched her purse tight to her body as though she carried with her a compendium of untold secrets. "I hope I'm not disturbing you, but I've been trying to call," she said, casting an eye about the darkened room as if searching for a just cause for her impromptu visit. "Left several messages on your phone."

He reached for the light switch on the wall and rubbed his face, his head hurting from the liquor. The look on her face told him she could smell it on his breath, too. "I've been a little busy."

"Everything okay? I haven't seen you in a while."

"I'm fine. Just busy, like I said."

Moss nodded and held his stare, as if waiting for more of the whys and wherefores. "I noticed it had been a couple of months since your last session, and I was in the area, so thought I'd come by and check in."

He said nothing for a long moment. "Can I get you something to drink?"

"Water's fine. Thank you."

He grabbed a clean glass from the cupboard and returned with the water. "Things are a little... *unusual* right now."

"So I hear," Moss said, sipping the water. "Got yourself some admirers outside, I see."

She was a woman that he had always admired since he'd known her. She had helped him through his darkest days after the accident that had taken his memory and carried off with whatever life had come before. Erin Moss was a good woman, and had treated him much the same. And for that alone, he owed her much, for she had become the only mainstay in his life since.

"Are you sure you're okay, Jacob?"

He nodded, then gestured for her to take a seat at the two-seater table. "I'm fine," he said. "Everybody keeps asking me."

"That's because everybody wants to know who Jacob Keller is. What you did goes a long way in these parts."

"A man died 'cause of what I did."

"You don't think you did the right thing?"

"No, I did the right thing. But he was still someone's son."

Moss nodded, a solemn look on her face. "Yes, he was."

Jacob cleared his throat and shook off the thought. "Do shrinks usually visit their patients like this?"

Moss sipped her water again, then placed the glass down on the table. "Only when they don't answer my calls."

He smiled. "I'd been meaning to call."

Moss sat back in her chair, her fingers locked together on her lap. "Do you want to talk about it?"

"About what?"

"The reason you're on the front page of every paper in the county."

"Nothing much to say," he said. "One's dead, and the other's got penance to do. They made their choice."

Moss tilted her head to one side with intrigue. "You believe that?"

"What do you mean?"

"You believe the men responsible deserve punishment for what happened?"

"Why wouldn't they?"

"I'm not saying they shouldn't. I'm saying there's always another way of looking at it."

"Seems like the only answer to me."

"Perhaps," Moss said, her voice softening now. "But none of us had any choice to be here. Other people made that decision for us, right?"

He looked hard at her. "Sure."

"In that case, you agree that we're all just the products of our parent's decisions. So what makes anyone think we have a choice about anything else we do in our lives?"

"You think those boys should be spared for what they did?"

Moss sipped her water again. "All I'm asking is a question. Are we all brought into this life as moral people corrupted by society? Or are we all born corrupted and tamed by it instead? Either way, punishment seems like a misguided idea as a bedrock for a moral society. It's based on righting wrongs and exacting revenge for things that, maybe, we have no control over."

"And you think there's a better option?"

Moss shrugged her shoulders. "Perhaps."

He considered her point carefully, then shook his head in dissent. "I believe humans are condemned to be free. Only *we* have the power to decide our actions, and *we* alone must be judged on what *we* do."

Moss was silent and half-smiling. "You've read Sartre?"

"A little," he said, and it was only then that he noticed Moss was drumming her index finger against the tabletop. A small quirk he had recognized over the years whenever she was about to broach a more difficult talking point.

"Are you still getting the dreams?" she said.

He drew in a breath and let the moment linger for a while. "Sometimes."

"The woman still?"

He nodded. "Mostly."

"And the headaches?"

"They come and go."

Moss finished her glass of water. "And what about memories? Has anything else come back to you?"

"I don't know," he said. "I have these images of what I think is my past. But they feel... distant, like they never really belonged to me."

"That's quite normal for someone who went through what you did," Moss said. "We've spoken about that before, remember?"

"I remember. It just made me realize that maybe life is nothing more than best guesses," he said, turning his head to look about the apartment as though he were a caged bird. "That we're all trapped in this space between the desire to know and the inability to fathom."

"I think that's very normal," Moss said. "It's our nature to try to understand the obscurities of our existence. But no one yet has found the answer." She retrieved a notepad and pen from her clutch bag, jotted something down, then teared the sheet loose.

Jacob looked down at the note that she handed to him. "What is this?"

"I want to try you on some new medication," said Moss. "It will help with the headaches."

He took the script, folded it up and put it in his chest pocket.

"I want you to come and see me every couple of weeks like you used to."

He looked off her stare and nodded. "I don't think that's necessary."

"I'm not asking."

He rolled his eyes and walked her to the door.

Moss looked up at him over the rims of her eyeglasses as she turned to him again. "I have one more request before I leave."

"What is it?"

Moss smiled. "Find yourself a woman, Jacob."

After he saw her out, he wandered back inside the apartment and sat alone for a while with the radio playing. As hard as he tried to fill his time with mindless things, there was only one thing that occupied his thoughts: the pretty woman he now knew as Amanda Wheeler and whose number he was staring at on the slip of paper that she had handed to him earlier that day. He'd thought about calling her all evening, but only now did he have enough liquor in him to act upon it. He picked up his cell and punched in the digits. A wearied voice answered.

"Hello?"

"Amanda?"

"Yes."

"It's Jacob. From the bus."

"I know," she said. Her voice was soft, and beneath the tiredness lied a renewed vigor. "What time is it?"

"Sorry, did I wake you?"

"I must have fallen asleep."

A silent moment passed between them. "Are you busy?"

"Right now?"

"Right now."

"No."

"Are you hungry?"

Another pause followed. "Sure, I could eat."

———

Cherrie's Corner Kitchen, like its namesake, was a dine-all-night eatery that occupied a small corner lot just three blocks from his apartment. He knew the place well enough, and Cherrie herself made sure her waitstaff reserved the same booth for him every Monday night when his refrigerator ran dry.

The place was quiet when he entered. Cherrie was standing behind the counter cleaning down the stove as he came in, then got straight to fixing him with a cup of coffee. Straight. Black. Strong. Just how he liked it.

Amanda was already sitting in one of the middle booths, warming her hands around her own cup of coffee that was still steaming and fresh from the pot. She looked up at him as he approached the booth and took the seat opposite. "It's nice here. Quiet," she said, looking about the place, taking in the stillness of a slow night. "My dad used to bring me here when I was little. It was called something different back then."

Before he'd removed his coat, Cherrie was at the table with his coffee and laid it down before him. She said nothing, but looked Amanda up and down where she sat, then winked her approval at him before leaving them to it.

"You know each other?" Amanda said, noticing the passing of silent words between him and the old woman.

He nodded. "I don't sleep too well, so I come here instead."

She leaned forward across the table. "Maybe it's the coffee keeping you awake."

He smiled. "You grew up here?"

"I did," she said, her eyes never leaving his. "My parents liked the simple life."

"And you don't?"

"I'm still working that out." She looked down at her hot coffee and stirred it with a spoon. "What's your story, Jacob?"

"Ain't got a story. Not here anyway. Guess you could say I'm a visitor."

"And how long you visiting for?"

He did the math. "Coming up two years now, I'd guess."

She smiled and studied his face, as if trying to search his soul for hidden truths. "They say there's two kinds of people that live here: those born here, and those running from something."

"Is that so?"

She offered a gentle nod. "So, what are you running from?"

He looked off her stare and down into his cup of coffee. "I wish I knew."

Amanda watched him through narrowed eyes, then smiled to herself. "I get it. You're the silent, mysterious type. Am I right?"

"No," he said. "I had an accident. Right before I came here."

"What kind of accident?"

"I crashed my truck."

"Sounds bad."

"Maybe. I don't remember it."

"You don't have much luck with trucks, do you?"

"Seems that way."

Amanda sat back in her seat with a furrowed brow. "You don't remember anything at all?"

He shook his head. "Not before it either."

The look on her face was one full of questions and concern alike.

"Don't worry," he said, offering a reassuring smile. "I'm fine now."

"I can't imagine what that's like."

"You get used to it. You can't miss what you don't know."

She shrugged her shoulders. "Why here?"

"Work mainly. I got some help with a place here once I got back on my feet."

"What about your family?"

"No family."

"Parents?"

"Like I said, no family. They died a long time ago, so I'm told. There's no one else."

She regarded him with heartbreak and horror in equal measure. "You don't remember your parents either?"

He shook his head with a vacant expression. "Not much, but enough about me. What about you?"

"What about me?"

"Who is Amanda Wheeler?"

She looked down and stirred her coffee again in slow and deliberate swirls. "Well, I like to be right about things. You should know that now. Don't like to admit when I'm wrong, either. My friends say I wear my heart on the outside. I'm rash. Sometimes quick-tempered. I have dreams bigger than my abilities. You already know I was born here and I'll probably die here unless I do something about it first."

He leaned back in his seat, surprised and yet charmed by her candor. "You don't like it here?"

"It's home," she said, with a tilt of the head. "But I want to make a different life for myself outside of this place. Not that my father understands that."

"What about your mother?"

Amanda pursed her lips as if trying to stifle a sob. "My mother is... not my mother anymore."

From the tremble in her voice, he sensed an unbearable weight of heartache and pain that spoke of a story that was better left for another day. "What are you studying?" he said.

She peered back up at him again with a puzzled shake of the head.

"On the bus..." he said. "You're always reading."

"I want to be a social worker. I use the ride to work to read." The glimmer of light in her eyes spoke only of a tenderhearted turn of mind.

"I think you'll be great."

"Really?" she said, her face pulled into one of suspicion now. "But you've only known me for, what, five minutes?"

"Sometimes that's all it takes."

She let out a small and retiring laugh. "I should warn you I come with baggage."

He met her stare across the table again. "You and everyone else, then."

"Maybe. What are you looking for?"

He sighed and leaned forward. "What do you mean?"

"You know," she said, looking out of the window at the darkened world that awaited them. "Out there?"

"Same as most, I guess. A reason."

They drank their coffees and sat and talked about everything and nothing at all until some ungodly hour when it was time to leave. When they quit the diner, he walked her to her car parked in the lot.

"You sure I can't give you a ride home?" she said.

"I like the walk. Clears my mind."

Amanda nodded and reached for the key in her purse. "You wanna do this again sometime?"

"Sure," he said, admiring the glistening black bodywork of the '72 Ford Torino as they approached the rear.

"It's my father's," Amanda said, noticing him looking at the car. "His pride and joy."

"Next to you, no doubt."

"Oh no. The car comes before me."

"And yet he still let you borrow it..."

Amanda beamed as she unlocked the Torino. "Oh, I almost forgot..." She reached into her purse again and handed him a book. "I forgot to give it back to you."

He looked down at the worn cover of Melville's *Moby Dick*.

"You left it on the bus," Amanda said.

"Thank you," he said, brushing her hand as he took the book. "I've been looking for this."

A silence passed between them. Amanda stood on the tips of her toes to kiss him on the cheek with all the tenderness he imagined she possessed. Then she was gone, into the black of the night, down the barren stretch of road towards the Eastside. And as he turned towards the empty sidewalk that awaited him, he spotted a lone black SUV parked across the street from the diner. It was parked as though it had been waiting for him, the driver's face scarcely lit behind the burning end of a cigarette.

Jacob watched from the corner under the streetlight. After a moment, the headlights of the SUV lifted and cut a beam through the darkness as the engine started. Then the vehicle turned in the road and vanished into the dark streets beyond.

Chapter 8

Jacob woke at first light, the slow rise of the low winter sun bringing with it another day more gray and miserable than the one before. With nothing else to do but sit and while away the hours, he showered and dressed and was out the door at sunup. He walked the three miles to the edge of town, his head turned down like a pilgrim in his march, the barren streets devoid of life at this hour. He arrived at the repair shop before opening, right on time to see a man in coveralls lifting the shutters for the day ahead. "Good morning."

"Is it?" the man said, his head tipped towards the grainy sky. His face was the color of aged cowhide from the years of unchecked sun, even in the winter months when there was none to be seen.

"Are you Mr. Wheeler?"

"Depends who's asking."

"Amanda said you might look at my truck for me."

"Did she now?" the man said as he approached. "That girl says a lot of things."

He stood before the man, looking up at his giant form that seemed to turn the morning darker still as he came towards him.

After the silence passed, the man laughed to himself as he reached for the switch on the wall to turn the lights on. "I'm just messin' with you, friend. My daughter said you'd be along." The man eyed him up and down as if sizing him up. "You're shorter than you look on that video."

"The good Lord gave me other talents," he said.

"I guess he did."

Jacob followed the man through the repair shop, across the oil-stained flagstones to a small office tucked away at the back.

"Have you got kids of your own?" the man asked.

"No, sir."

The man threw on an old threadbare jac-shirt hanging on a wall peg and rolled up the sleeves to his forearms. "Well, maybe one day you'll understand how much I can't thank you enough for what you did."

Jacob stood silent, and in him he felt nothing but embarrassment at the compliment.

"I'll get a tow out to you later today," the man said.

"Thank you," he said, reaching into his pocket to dig out the wad of loose banknotes.

The man pressed his glasses back on his face and looked hard at him, as if offended by the sight of cash presented to him. "Did you listen to a word I just said?"

"I don't expect a handout." Jacob said, his hand outstretched with the cash still.

"Good, because I don't give 'em," the man replied. "Now put your money away, son."

Jacob returned the notes to his pocket. After a minute, he turned to leave.

"You got somewhere else to be?" the man said.

Jacob looked back over his shoulder. The man was still stood there watching him. "Excuse me?"

"I heard you're looking for work?"

"Uh... well," he said, stumbling over his words.

"Well, are ya or ain't ya?"

"Yes, sir."

"My daughter says you got experience with machines?"

Jacob looked about the floor lined with engine parts and loose bodywork. "Not this kind."

"Nevermind. You'll pick it up," the man said, handing him the spare tool bag atop the shelf and sizing him up again where he stood. "There's a spare boilersuit in the back which should fit. I pay eighty-five a day to start. Job's yours if you want it."

He shook the man's hand and only then did he realize he still had no name for his new boss. "Thank you, sir."

"You call me Hank," the man said, his grip like a vise as they shook hands. "Listen to what I tell ya, and we'll get along just fine."

———

At noon, Jacob stepped out to get some air to rid himself of the stench of engine fumes and the taste of oil in his mouth. He stood squinting with his head tilted to the colorless sky and thought that he could be in worse places in the world right now. In fact, this line of work suited him just fine, and Amanda's father was a man he admired upon first meeting. Hank Wheeler was as honest as the day was long, and, in time, he figured he could earn the old man's respect. Not just because of what he did for his daughter—which was nothing much to be fair—but because he would give the man the hard hours deserving of the good turn which had been vouchsafed to him.

Jacob drank his warm coffee and looked back down to the world anew, and surveyed the row of ruined buildings in front of him. As he cast a long glance across the street, he took pause at the sight of the black SUV, parked up by the side of the road in front of the old food processing plant opposite the body shop. The same black SUV he had seen the night before outside the diner. The same black figure watching him from behind the wheel as though his life was playing out like the main feature for all to witness.

Jacob swallowed down the rest of his coffee and walked to the end of the apron, marking the boundary of the body shop. He stood and watched the driver from a distance, and the unseen driver sat and watched him in return. It was only at the blare of a horn that he peeled his eyes away from the road ahead and found Hank waving him over from inside the body shop.

"She's purring like a kitten now," said Hank, closing the hood on his Ford Bronco that was now idling in the repair bay. "A new carburetor and fuel line. That's why you had no power. She should be good to go again."

Jacob tipped his head in gratitude.

Hank wiped the oil off his hands with an old rag and tossed Jacob the keys. "Put a full tank of gas in for you as well, but I want no thanks for that." Hank stretched his back, the years of grind and toil taking its toll on the old man's bones. "You finished breaking?"

Jacob looked back over his shoulder to see that the spot where the black SUV had been parked was now empty again.

"Everything okay?" said Hank.

"Yeah. It's fine."

"Good, then let's get back to work already."

———

The darkness had arrived by quitting time and the sky was as black as an oil spill turning above his head. There was a missed call from Amanda on his cellphone when he returned to his truck, now running again like a salvaged vessel ready for one last voyage. He called Amanda back and pressed the phone to his ear.

"I hear you got a new job." Her voice was soft and unhurried, as though she had done nothing but await his call.

"Word travels fast."

"Yes, it does. Are you free tonight? I thought we could pick up where we left off."

"Sure," he said. "You like pasta?"

"Of course."

"Eight-thirty, my place?"

"See you then."

And with that, she was gone again.

He drove the long way home, past the darkened haunts of the town's inebriates and laboring men who came together after a hard day's work to drink and shoot the breeze and rebuild their spirits, ready to do the same thing all over again tomorrow.

Off the main drag, he turned down a quieter street and crawled past Seymour's Tavern, spotting the usual faces at the bar through the window as he pulled into a bay outside.

All heads seemed to turn to him as he entered, as though he had disturbed this inner sanctum, saved only for the hardened drinkers among them. But as soon as he lifted his eyes to the unwelcomed silence, a round of applause went up, as though he had returned from some wretched battle as a triumphant king to his newfound glory.

He stepped in and looked about the faces amongst the hollers and whistles of those standing with their hands clasped in slow applaud. All but one man stood for him as he came forward. The silent critic remained seated with his back to him and drank his fill as though he were deaf to the hue and cry around him.

"There's that crazy sonofabitch," said one voice, but he couldn't tell man from man amongst the roughened crowd.

And then the scrawny frame of Leland Hawes stepped forward from the back. "Wes, get this man a cold beverage. He's earned it."

Wes Brooks, the barkeep of this particular concern, lifted his head from across the bar and reached for a clean glass off the shelf. "It's been a month of Sundays since I last saw you in here. Was starting to wonder if you were ever minded to pay that tab of yours."

"Don't worry, Wes. I got it covered," he said as he approached the bar through a chain of backslapping.

"The usual?" Wes said, already pouring the beer into the empty glass.

He nodded and pulled up a stool next to the loner, who hadn't moved an inch and was now sitting with his head down, looking into his tumbler of whisky as though it were some oracle's scrying glass.

"You won't find any favor with me, kid, so don't waste your time trying," the loner said.

"I wasn't looking for any."

"Good, then you won't mind leaving me alone." The loner drank his liquor and wiped his mouth dry on his shirtsleeve.

Everyone knew the man's name. He'd been a foremost feature of this fine establishment since he'd retired as sheriff some ten years ago, the wooden bar now worn in the exact spot where his elbows rested, which was no coincidence, for he was ever-present and yet remained undisturbed, much the like the years of dust that had gathered in the corners of the splintered sills. To those that knew him, he answered to *Abel*. Everyone else left him well alone.

"Can I get you another?" he said.

Abel looked sideways at him and laughed. "You think you're smart?"

Jacob shook his head as Wes returned with his cold beer and laid it down on the bar. "I just asked if you wanted a drink."

"I ain't deaf," Abel said. "And I see right through you just fine, too."

"See what?"

"You think you're better than me."

"I never said that."

"Didn't need to. It's written all over your shit-eating face."

Jacob turned off Abel's stare as the bar went quiet, suddenly alert to the raised voice that rarely spoke from the corner. The man was spoiling for a fight, but he gave him no further excuse for one. "Forget I asked."

"We don't need no vigilantes running amuck around here." Abel stepped down off his stool and turned to face him now, unsteady on his feet, the smell of liquor strong on his breath. "I'm talking to you."

Jacob laid down his glass and kept his gaze fixed firmly on Wes, whose eyes were now darting back and forth between the two men. "I said forget it."

"That's enough, *Abel*," Wes said, saying his piece

before the drunkard could spit another word. "The kid did right, which is more than you ever did."

The room fell quiet for a long while, then Abel slid his empty tumbler to one side and stood again and took his leave under the silence of all. As soon as he was gone, the place filled with the usual din of a merry crowd.

"Eight-ball, Jack?" Leland said, chalking the tip of the cue as he came forward.

"Maybe later," he said.

Leland nodded. "Alright. Winner plays our very own *Valiant Jack* over here. Place your bets."

Jacob pulled up a seat at the bar and drank his beer alone, with nothing but his thoughts for company. No one disturbed him. There was an unspoken rule that when a man sat at the bar, he was to be left to himself, and so it came as some surprise when he suddenly felt someone else beside him, their presence like a lingering shadow.

Wes glanced up from behind the bar as the stranger approached. "Can I get you something, fella?"

The stranger leaned in and Jacob could smell Old Spice amongst the stench of Brylcreem.

"Same he's having," the stranger said, his black hair slicked with precision.

Jacob turned in his seat and met the stranger's quizzical look from behind his tinted glasses.

The stranger offered a half-smile in greeting as he took up the stool next to him. "I hope the beer tastes better than the place looks," he said, casting an eye about the joint.

Jacob shrugged and took a slug of beer and kept to

himself, not wishing to invite any further comment from this peculiar entrant. Wes returned with the stranger's beer, then moved off again.

The stranger took a sip and exhaled. "New Brunswick. Not the kinda place I'd imagined you'd be."

Jacob tilted his head to one side as he studied the man. "Sorry, do we know each other?"

"I don't know. You tell me."

"Listen, if you're a reporter... I'm not talking."

"I saw the video."

"Which paper are you with?"

The stranger let out a laugh as strange as the familiarity with which he had approached him. "C'mon, Patrick, you can quit the act now."

"Excuse me?"

They held each other's stare for a long moment and the stranger held up his hands as though embracing a long departed friend. "I know it's been a while, but I haven't aged that much."

Jacob regarded him with a blank expression, at a loss to place the stranger's name or face, neither of which was familiar to him at all. "I'm sorry, I don't know—"

"It's me. Rick." The stranger removed his glasses as though the black of his eyes held the answer to any doubt.

Try as he might, and as discomfited as he ought to be, he felt nothing but ignorance at the presence of the man before him. All he could do was shake his head, nonplussed by the whole affair. And then, from the far end of the room, he heard his means of escape.

"Your up, Jack. Get your ass over here!"

His neck snapped round at the sound of his name. From across the room, he spotted Leland setting up the pool table for another round. He stood, proffered a hand to the stranger, and took up his half-drunk beer with the other. "Jack Keller."

The stranger looked hard at him as they shook hands. "Sorry. Must have got you confused with someone else."

Jacob tipped his head as he moved off towards the others gathered around the pool table. "Enjoy the beer."

"Yeah, thanks," the stranger said.

Chapter 9

They ate by candlelight on his cheap two-seater table. Just the two of them. Two bowls of pasta and two bottles of Blue Ribbon between them, their occasional glances caught between the melodies of Delta blues playing on the radio.

He ate like a man who savored each moment, and she ate at a pace unbecoming of any other woman he knew. And yet, with her, it seemed like an endearing habit of a lifetime.

"Sorry," Amanda said, comparing her empty plate to his half-eaten one. "I've always been a fast eater."

"I guess I should take it as a compliment."

"Blame it on my mother. She always used to make us hurry our dinner so she could put us to bed before she went back to work for the night."

He looked up at her as he forked in another morsel. "There's plenty more if you want it?"

She regarded him with a coquettish smile and slid her plate to one side. "I was saving room for something else."

He held her stare for a long moment, noticing her bottle of beer was also empty. A woman of his own heart. "Another beer instead?"

"I've got legs," she said, getting to her feet before he could. "But just so you know, I'm impervious to alcohol."

"Wasn't trying to get you drunk."

"Of course you weren't," she said, smiling as she crossed the room and grabbed two more bottles from the refrigerator. When she returned, she sat and sipped her beer, eyed his bandaged arm up and down, then his chest where it was slightly open at the collar, the hint of black ink just below his collarbone. "What does your tattoo mean?"

He glanced down at the trails of black ink made with an ungainly hand and unbuttoned his shirt to reveal the faded markings: a stiletto dagger pierced through a shamrock. "I don't remember."

She considered it for a moment. "Are you Irish?"

He leaned forward across the table. "I don't think so."

Amanda nodded, then looked up at him with a deadened expression. "Some say the shamrock symbolizes the holy trinity. Others say it stands for hope, faith, and love."

"That a fact?"

"Yes, it is."

"And the dagger?"

"Treachery," she said as she lifted her eyes to meet his again. "Or sacrifice. Depends who you ask."

"How do you know this?"

"I read about it somewhere. It's called semiotics."

"Semi-*what*?"

"Nevermind. You'll just have to trust me."

They shared a laugh. Jacob sipped his beer and finished up his plate. "You ever considered teaching instead?"

"I was a terrible student as a kid. Besides, I don't have the patience for it."

"But you're a student now..."

"It's hard," she said, and the change on her face was almost immediate. A heavy sigh followed the heave of her shoulders. "Between work and, well, everything else."

"Your mom?" he asked, treading lightly, but spotting the unspoken sense that she was at ease to recount whatever was on her mind.

"Yes, my mother."

At once he could see her body tense and shrink at the mention of it, like some frightened animal trembling in the ground cover. He said nothing, just waited for her to find her voice again.

"She has dementia," she said, the faintest crack as she spoke. "She barely recognizes me anymore. I see her every Saturday."

"And your father?"

She shook her head like a parent disappointed in their only child. "He doesn't see her. Says it's too hard for him." Her lips curled in a humorless smile. "Like it's any easier for me. The man has no idea."

"When did he last see her?"

"I lost count of the days."

Jacob looked down at the gold necklace around her neck. The one she had so fiercely defended on the bus that morning, as though it were an extension of her very self. On the end hung a circular pendant with the delicate embossed letters of a name still visible in the failing light. "Who's *Katie*?"

Amanda swallowed dry and gripped the pendant in one palm, all her vulnerabilities exposed in that single act. "You like all the tough questions, huh?"

"I just want to get to know you."

She held his stare for a moment, then smiled again, as if recounting a bittersweet memory. "She was my sister."

All he could do was watch as she sat looking vacantly at her empty plate, as though a thousand images of her forgotten past had been summoned all at once. "I'm sorry," he said.

"It's okay." Her eyes softened at whatever memories that remained. "It was a long time ago." Amanda caught the sob and sat back, looking around the room, her eyes settling on the wall of books lined up at one end. "You like to read?"

"Sure," he said.

She stood and went over to the bookshelf and started browsing the titles on the spines. Her finger settled on one in particular as she removed it from the shelf and studied the cover of Hemingway's *The Old Man and the Sea* with familiarity. "I know this one."

"Yeah?"

"They made us read it in our senior year. Some man who tries to catch a big fish and comes back with nothing. I never understood the point of it."

He smiled to himself and remained seated. "It's not about coming back with nothing."

"Uh, huh? Then what's it about?"

"The old man caught the fish," he said, recounting the story. "It was the greatest catch of his life."

"That never happened."

"Sure did. Then he lashed it to his boat. But the fish bled out in the water on the way home. The sharks smelled blood and, well, you know the rest."

"They ate it?"

"Right."

"So, he came back with nothing. Like I said, a waste of time."

"Depends how you look at it."

"What do you mean?"

"The old man fought harder than he'd ever done to catch that fish. And even when he came home with nothing but his boat, he was still content."

"How so?"

"Because his spirit was undefeated. Because no man is made for defeat in this world. That's why."

Amanda rolled her eyes. "How romantic."

Jacob stood and offered his outstretched palm. "Do you dance?"

She put the book down on the coffee table and came

close to him, her body against his as he held her waist with his free hand. They swayed gently to the melody on the radio as she followed his lead. He could smell the scent of her perfume as he held her closer still, subtle yet sweet to the senses. They kept their eyes fixed upon one another, as if each were trying to search for the other's soul that lurked behind their mortal existence. And as she raised a smile at him, he leaned down and kissed her. And she kissed him all the same, as though the seconds had melted into a time-less void where nothing else existed but them and them alone. He caressed her neck with the tips of his fingers as she unbuttoned his shirt, one at a time, as they stumbled forward against the wall. The warmth of her breath hurried against his cheek. He kissed her again, but this time her lips were unmoving, as though all feeling had suddenly slipped from her rigid body.

"Shit!" she said.

"What?"

"There's someone at the window."

He pulled back at once, his shirt hanging off him as he turned to follow her gaze fixed upon the rear door where the drapes had yet to be drawn.

"Who is that?" Amanda said, recoiling at the sight of the small face of a boy pressed against the glass, looking in at them with an absent expression, like a child who under-stood the ways of the world before his time.

"It's Ben," he said, buttoning up his shirt again.

Amanda swallowed, trying to catch her breath again. "You never said you had a kid."

"I don't," he replied, walking to the door to let the boy in from the cold. "He lives upstairs."

Amanda straightened her blouse and averted her gaze as the boy came in.

"What are you doing out there?" he said.

"Nothing," said the boy.

"Didn't look like nothing."

Ben looked up at him, then pointed. "Who's she?"

"This is Amanda," he said, inviting her to come forward.

"Is she your girlfriend?"

He didn't know how to answer that. "Have you eaten?"

The boy shook his head.

"There's some leftover in the pan over there. You can warm it up in the microwave."

The boy shuffled over to the kitchen counter in silence and filled his plate from the pan of pasta that had gone cold.

When Jacob turned back, he saw Amanda stood awkwardly to one side, like a woman caught in the act of impropriety. He came close to her and whispered. "I'm sorry," he said. "I let him hang out here from time to time."

She regarded him with an oddly vacant look, understanding of the boy's ease in his presence, and yet not understanding the situation at all. "But he's not yours?"

Jacob shook his head. "He lives upstairs, like I said. His aunt... let's just say she could do better looking after him. He's a good kid."

Amanda took a moment, then drew in a sharp breath. "Okay. It wasn't what I was expecting," she said, "but let's go with it."

As he turned again, he noticed the boy had crept back into the center of the room holding a deck of cards in one hand and looking up at Amanda with all the wonder that only a child possessed.

"You know how to play five-card draw?" Ben said.

Amanda shook her head.

"It's okay," the boy replied, reaching for her hand. "I can teach you."

———

The boy fell asleep in her arms on the couch as they saw out the rest of their night in front of the television. Amanda was right. It wasn't how he expected this night to end either, but it had been the best night he could remember in some while.

Amanda gently eased Ben from her embrace and rested his head on the cushion as she stood and grabbed her coat from the back of the chair. "I should go," she said.

He rose to join her. "Sure. I understand." He followed her out into the hallway and walked her to the door.

"It's not because of Ben," she said. "Well, it is, but it's for the right reason."

He smiled as she leaned in to kiss him on the cheek. "He likes you."

Amanda beamed, yet her eyes were weary. "I like him, too."

He opened the door on to a dark night. "Does your father know?"

Amanda shook her head. "I'm a big girl. I don't need my father's permission to date somebody."

"Sure, but I'm working with the man."

"I won't tell if you don't." A coquettish smile creeped across her mouth as she stepped out and pulled her collar up about her neck against the biting wind. "Goodnight, Jacob."

"Goodnight," he said as he watched her leave. The moment felt strange to him, unable to place the knot in his stomach. He figured he must have kept the company of women in whatever life he could no longer remember, but how he felt now was new to him, as though he were courting for the first time. Not that he hadn't been interested before now. There had been a few conquests to pass the lonely nights along the way. But what he'd never felt was a connection with someone worth pursuing beyond the carnal pleasures. Until now.

The boy lay curled up on the couch with his eyes closed when he returned, dead to the world and all its horrors. He retrieved an old patchwork eiderdown from the closet, laid it over the boy, then retired to his own bed for the night, ready for the nightmares that awaited him.

Tomorrow was another day, and yet, for the first time in as long as he could remember, it was one that he had every reason to wake for.

Chapter 10

He woke again in the damp of his bedsheets, his room dark beyond dark, unsure of anything but the face of the nameless woman that haunted his dreams without end. The night terrors had grown no less frequent over the years. Some nights were worse than others, but each night he feared the onset of tiredness as the darkness drew in, and the image of her stricken countenance that plagued his unconscious mind like a roaming ghost lost on its way to the promised land. He knew nothing about her except that she had meant something to him in whatever life had come before, as though all her secrets lied behind the locked doors of the prison of his forgotten memories. All he knew was that, somewhere, she was waiting for him, lost in a world that existed between the waking one and whatever faculty that lied beyond it.

He got up and poured himself a glass of water from the kitchen, tracing the faint light from the lamp that he'd left on in the hallway. The boy was still asleep on the couch, and he neither stirred nor made a sound. He stepped outside to cool his body, the sweat on the nape of his neck now cold to the touch, and as he looked long across the street, he spotted a black dog roaming the lifeless gardens like a stray without a home. The dog stopped to look at him, its eyes almost electric against the black of its fur, then scarpered amongst the underbrush. As he glanced up again, he saw something else. The black SUV parked up at the side of the road five houses down with its lights off. The same car he had seen on no less than two separate occasions. At this distance, it was impossible to tell if the driver was present, but the sight of it again spurred an idea.

Jacob finished his water and looked about the darkened windows of the houses in front of him. Only some showed signs of life, the rest left to rot in their abandonment. The foreclosure signs lined up like flagstaffs of a stone-broke nation. He wandered back inside his apartment and left the empty glass of water on the side table as he started for the rear door. He unlocked it and left it ajar, then cut across the yard and scaled the fence in silence. The rear exit out of the apartment block backed on to a narrow alleyway that spilled out onto the adjacent street. He followed it round, tracing the rear of the vacant houses until he could see the black SUV through a gap between the hedgerows on the other side. The driver never saw him coming as he heaved the door open and pulled the figure to the ground, his knee pressed firmly into the side of the driver's neck as he grappled to lock up an arm. The driver grunted, pinioned to the ground and unable to move.

"Who the hell are you?" Jacob said, keeping just enough weight off the man's neck to allow him to breathe. It was only when his eyes focused under the streetlights that he noticed that the man lying with his face in the dirt was the stranger that had spoken to him in that bar earlier that evening and whose name he'd already forgotten.

The stranger struggled to get his words out, his lungs fighting for whatever air they could rescue. "Let... me... up!"

"Why are you following me?"

"I just... want.... to talk."

Jacob eased off the man's neck and hoisted him up, pressing his spine hard against the side of the SUV. "Talk about what? I don't know you."

The stranger raised his hands in submission, then looked at him with an expression that carried nothing but honest-to-God fear. "You're not safe here."

Jacob backed away, letting the man have his space. He was no threat to him. "I'll ask again, who are you?"

The stranger brushed down the dirt off his coat and straightened himself. "I already told you," he said, massaging the side of his neck. "It's Rick."

"Why are you here?"

"You really don't remember me?"

Jacob repeated the question. "Why are you here?"

The stranger looked hard at him. "For you."

"I don't know you."

The stranger stepped forward to meet him under the dim glow of the streetlights overhead, studying his face through narrowed and heavy-lidded eyes. "It is you. I know it is," he said. "But you don't remember me?"

"I've never seen you before today," he said.

The stranger stepped back as he reached into his pocket for a pack of cigarettes, his face glowing as he lit the end. "We used to run together. In Philly. Jimmy Lynch's crew."

He looked at him with a deadened expression, giving him nothing. But on hearing the name, he felt something inside of him stir into consciousness, like some echo from the past that had found its way back again.

"What happened to you, Patrick?" the stranger asked.

"My name is Jacob," he said, kneading the pain in his arm through the layers of gauze.

The stranger puffed his smoke and leveled with him. "Your face is all over the news. It won't take them long to find you, either. And when they do—"

Jacob pressed a hard palm into the stranger's chest, sending him backwards against the side of the parked SUV again. "If I see you outside my apartment again—or anywhere—I'll make sure you remember my name next time." He left the stranger to finish his smoke and wandered back towards his apartment, the night growing colder by the minute and the tops of the cars now covered in a heavy frost. As he approached the end of the sidewalk, he heard the stranger call out to him a last time.

"Patrick?"

He turned to see the man stub out his cigarette, then pull down his shirt collar to reveal the faded ink above his heart. A shamrock and a dagger just like his own. He stood and watched as the stranger climbed back into the SUV and drove off into the black of the night.

Chapter 11

The boy was gone when he woke the next morning, an empty spot on the couch where he had left him the night before, the eiderdown folded in a neat square and left to one side as though he had never been there. He found it odd that the boy, as young as he was, adopted an orderliness unexpected of his years. And yet, in the same breath, it made complete sense. Perhaps it was the boy's only way of maintaining control in his life, where there was nothing else but mayhem and abandonment.

When he went back to the bedroom to get dressed, he noticed a slip of paper lying flat on the doormat in the hallway, a line of digits on one side he recognized as a cellphone number, and beneath that a simple note scrawled with an ill-formed hand.

I know it's you.

When he turned it over in his hand, he saw it was not just a note at all, but a photograph, worn at the corners and creased in the middle as though it once belonged in a billfold.

The picture was old, clear from the hairless chin of the man he recognized as himself in a time he could not place, and the muted colors of the image that had faded from the years. He was smiling with the happiness and humor of a man he did not recognize, and next to him stood a woman with a smile to match. But this was not just any woman. It was *her*, the nameless woman that haunted his nights. She looked the same, except her eyes were absent of their usual wretchedness. And from the way she draped her arms over his shoulders, he knew then that this woman had once been someone to him, and not merely a figment of his nightmares.

Jacob let his eyes wander the image for a moment, for there were not just two people in the photograph, but three: himself, the nameless woman, and the stranger, who was stood on his other side. The one who had been following him. Each of them from a time that was unknown to him, but a time in which they were all once acquainted. It had always been his greatest fear. That one day, something or someone from his unremembered past would come back to find him.

He placed the photograph to one side as the screen on his cellphone lit up. A text from Amanda.

I enjoyed last night with you.

He messaged her back, then got showered and dressed for work.

———

"Why do I get the impression you're not paying attention?"

Jacob looked up at Hank Wheeler, who was bent at the waist under the hood of a truck, the downward tilt on the old man's mouth a display of his ill-humor as he held out a palm like a beggarman seeking alms. "Sorry," he said, passing him the socket wrench. The old man was right. His mind had been wandering.

Hank came out from under the hood and stretched his back. "I've seen that look before," he said, giving him the once over. "Seems like a woman's work to me."

Jacob swallowed dry. He was certain that the old man was unaware that his daughter had been at his apartment the night before, but Amanda was the least of his concerns. "You're married?"

"Is that a question?"

"I guess."

Hank nodded as he sipped his coffee. "Thirty-nine years."

"All good ones?"

The old man took a moment to answer that, his face a picture of heartsore weariness. "Thirty five, at least."

"And the rest?"

"Patti ain't so well these days." Hank cleared his throat to silence the sob.

"I'm sorry," he said. Although he already knew of the man's pain from his daughter, he sensed the wound cut much deeper than she had let on.

"It's okay," Hank said, pulling back his shoulders and standing tall. "The good Lord ain't been kind to my wife. Her brain's been eating her away for years. She ain't the woman I married all those years ago. Not anymore."

"You still love her, though?"

Hank looked hard at him with his deep-set eyes and creased brow as he perched on the end of the workbench. "Of course I do. She's still my wife," he said. "Sometimes I just feel like everything we lived for was for nothing. That everything that happened between us doesn't matter anymore. Like there's a part of me left behind in some other place. In some other time."

They sat there for a long moment, listening to the rain coming down, neither man knowing how to fill the silence.

"I don't expect you to understand," said Hank.

"No," he said. "I do."

Hank looked out at the gray and lifeless world outside. Nothing but cold rain dancing on the blacktop. "You believe in evil?"

"I don't think good can exist without the possibility of evil."

"That may be true." The old man's eyes were filled with tears, yet he didn't cry. "Anyway, enough about that. You gonna tell me what's on your mind or not?"

"I'm not really sure what it is yet."

"Someone botherin' you?"

"I don't think so. Just somebody from my past."

Hank put a hand on his shoulder and stood again as the phone in the office rang. "Life is plenty hard on its own, son. You don't need anybody else making it harder for you."

Jacob nodded, then stood with the old man as the phone rang on. "You want me to get that?"

Hank shook his head and took up the socket wrench. "I've been here for twenty years. Anyone who needs me knows where to find me."

"Then why do you have a phone?"

Hank looked down at him and smiled. "Because Patti made me," he said. "She never used to leave me alone."

For all his might and fine fettle, he thought that old Hank Wheeler was not the man of cold indifference that his daughter had painted. Behind the sturdiness lied not a heart of stone, but a heart of pulp that had hardened through years of lament. It was how he got through his days in this life. It was how he found a reason to keep going, working every hour he could, between the unanswered calls that reminded him of his wife that once was. This was how he remembered her.

———

At sundown, they packed up their things and locked up for the night. When Jacob returned to his truck, he saw the folded photograph hidden amongst the old liquor store receipts inside the console tray. He sat and studied the photograph with the cabin light on, trying to put his mind to work. But there was nothing familiar about it. No time or sense of place. On the back, he found the note and the number again. He studied the digits carefully. A part of him wanted to know. Another part wanted no such thing at all. He reached for his cell and dialed the number, anyway.

The stranger's roughened voice answered his call. "Yeah?"

"What's her name?" he asked, dispensing with the usual pleasantries.

"Excuse me?"

"The woman in the picture you left on my doorstep. Who is she?"

Silence. Then the stranger followed with an answer. "Alice," he said, as though the name should mean something. "Your wife."

He felt his chest tighten upon hearing the name, like someone had placed his heart in a vise and turned the screws. Somewhere, he had always known that the memories of the nameless woman were as real as she was. And now he had a name for her, too.

The stranger's voice called back to him. "Are you still there?"

He inhaled sharply and looked at himself in the rearview, his face tired and drawn as the day itself. "We need to talk."

Chapter 12

"Back so soon?"

Jacob glanced up as he entered the diner to see Cherrie stood with a pot of coffee in her hand. The place was as dead as ever for a weeknight, and the rain that was falling in sheets did nothing to help. "I'm meeting someone here."

Cherrie smiled her crooked smile as he came forward and shook down his wet coat. "That lady friend of yours again?"

"Someone else."

"Oh. You dirty dog."

"It's not like that."

"It's a free country, sugar," she said, getting back to work behind the counter. "Besides, you're just about the only one keeping me in business these days."

He looked about the place and the few faces who greeted his presence with knowing glances, then made his way to his usual booth at the far end of the diner, only to find another man sat in his seat, licking his fingers dry and wiping his mouth with a napkin as he finished his plate of eggs and bacon.

The trucker peered up at him as he combed his beard between his fingers, his eyes deep-set beneath the peak of his ball cap. "Can I help you?"

He said nothing at all, just stood looking down at the bearded man from the aisle.

"Find a seat," Cherrie said, appearing beside him now, his displeasure not going unnoticed by the old woman as a silent understanding passed between them. "Coffee's on me tonight."

He found another booth by the far window, away from earshot of anyone who cared to listen, then reached into his coat pocket to find the folded photograph. He studied it again, as if expecting to see something different, as though whatever he'd forgotten would suddenly emerge from the locus of his mind. But nothing came but the empty void of his unremembered past.

It had taken him some time to call to mind what little he could after the accident. Nothing but fragments of memories of his youth. He held only the faintest of memories of his mother and the way she brushed his hair as a boy. He thought he remembered his father too, but more the smell of whiskey on his breath when he held him at night. He could not recall the last time he had seen them, for both his parents existed as nothing more than subtle brush strokes on an aging canvas, their faces no older than his own now. From what memories he could muster, his mother had been a kind woman, and his father a man of moral repute. He had loved them like any child loves their parents, but inside him lied an inescapable distance, as though the waning echoes of them would not allow for sentiment, for most of his memories were nothing more than missing pieces of an unfinished puzzle.

Cherrie appeared at the table with his pot of hot coffee and a scrapple sandwich, then wandered back to the counter. He sat and drank his coffee and watched the rain lash down outside and the lights of passing cars come and go into the darkness. When he looked up again, the minute hand on the wall clock had moved a half-turn, yet there was still no sign of the stranger. He checked his cellphone. No messages or missed calls. He sat and waited a few more minutes before Cherrie returned with another pot of fresh coffee.

"I'd say you've been stood up, sugar," she said.

Jacob looked outside again to an empty parking lot. "Seems that way."

"You want a refill?"

He shook his head and got to his feet. "Gotta use the John, then I'll be on my way."

"Okay, but I don't want any mess back there. I just cleaned the place."

He took up his cellphone as he started for the restroom and dialed the last number he'd called. It rang out to the stranger's voicemail. He took a leak, then splashed his face with cold water from the faucet and patted it dry with a paper towel from the dispenser. Then the hairs on the back of his neck stood on end, like a dog's raised hackles, as he heard the scream.

He followed the hollering back out into the main diner. Cherrie was standing at the corner of the serving counter, jaw slack and face ashen, her eyes fixed to the entrance. Next to her, a father shielded his young daughter's eyes with a cupped hand at the sight of the stranger coming through the door, his eyes like glowing coals, wide and wild, blood pouring through the gaps in his fingers wrapped around his throat. The stranger staggered forward as he caught sight of him, clutching his neck as if afraid to let go but trying to speak at the same time, his eyes so big they looked fit to fall from their sockets. The stranger's left arm was covered in blood, and as he collapsed to his knees, his arms flopped beside him, releasing a spray of arterial gore that covered the walls, the formica tables, the vinyl floor. Soon there was blood everywhere.

Jacob hurried to his side and squatted, then placed his hands around the man's throat to stem the bleeding. "Call somebody!" he said.

Cherrie reached for the phone as the man buckled and writhed in his arms and, before long, the man was floundering in a pool of his own blood.

The stranger tried to speak again but couldn't get the words out, only the gargle of yet more blood in the back of his mouth, a clean slice right through the carotid.

The stranger was dead within the minute, his body still and lifeless, his eyes glassy and unmoving, as though he were staring at something small on the ground. Yet the blood kept coming.

Jacob released his grip on the man's throat, his hands covered in the man's blood. And as he stepped back, he noticed the stranger's coat fall open, his wallet half-exposed in the inner pocket, a pistol holstered to his side.

"My God," Cherrie said, "is he dead?"

Jacob didn't bother to look up. "Get everyone out of here." As the few patrons emptied out, he squatted again beside the man's dead body and reached a hand into his coat pocket to retrieve his billfold. Cash. Cards. A Pennsylvania driver's licence. He removed the licence, then stood again and studied the face and details on the front: *Rick Reynolds. Born on the 31st of December 1975.*

The face meant nothing to him, but at least he had a name.

———

"You have a habit of finding yourself in the wrong place at the wrong time, Mr. Keller." Chief Morales eyeballed him as they stood outside the diner, the rain having quelled to a fine spit.

Two deputies cordoned off the entrance with yellow tape as the paramedics returned to their ambulance with an empty gurney. The stranger's dead body left where he fell.

Jacob cleaned the blood off his face with a damp cloth

and perched on the wall outside, next to the stranger's black SUV.

The chief offered him a cigarette. "Did you know him?"

"I don't smoke," he said. "And no, I didn't know him."

Morales lit a cigarette for himself and took a long drag. "But you were waiting for him, right?"

He nodded. "Yes, but I didn't know him."

The chief peered at him through his small and narrowed eyes as the streetlights cast a hard shadow across his worn and haggard face. "You understand why I might find that hard to believe?"

"Trust me, it's harder to explain."

"Well, you best start trying."

Jacob sat there, holding the bloody rag in his hand as he tried to find the words to explain it all. The more he thought about it, the crazier it sounded in his head. He was here to a meet a man of whom he knew nothing, and yet, that same man had now turned up with his neck sliced from end to end. *Crazy* was a euphemism. The whole thing sounded like rank fiction. "I didn't know him," he said.

Morales took another drag on his cigarette, then pointed to the black SUV. "You said that's his vehicle?"

He nodded.

The chief leaned down to steal a glance through the window of the vehicle. "How is it you know this car belongs to a man you claim not to know? A man you agreed to meet here tonight, might I add?"

Jacob fell silent, his mind working double-time to contrive a reason to dispel the chief's suspicion.

"Do you make a habit of meeting people you don't know, Mr. Keller?"

He averted his gaze, feigning discomfort. Then a thought occurred to him. "Sometimes."

The chief looked at him in silence, then a look passed over his face as though he wished he had never asked at all. "Oh, I see," he said, the realization of the encounter now apparent to him. "You were…"

"We only exchanged a brief phone call," he said, yielding to the chief's false theory. It gave him no pleasure, but it was enough to douse any suspicion.

Morales cleared his throat and stubbed out his cigarette to fill the silence. "How did you become… acquainted?"

"Seymour's. He was there the other night. Said he was passing through."

"Did he say where he was staying?"

Jacob shook his head. That was a truth. In fact, he hadn't told a single lie. He just hadn't bothered to correct the chief's misreading of the situation, which was that he was here to meet a stranger to exchange favors of a certain kind that, to the chief at least, were beyond the pale.

"And I don't suppose you know why anyone would have cause to kill this man?"

He looked Morales dead in the eye. "Like I said, we only exchanged a couple of words."

The chief reached into his pocket for another cigarette

as though the long night before him was just starting. "You best get yourself home and cleaned up. But I'll be needing another statement from you in the morning."

Jacob stood and left the bloody rag on the wall, then returned to his truck. Through the rearview, he watched the chief watching him as he banked a right out of the parking lot, heading home. Another day behind him. Another question to answer.

Who was Rick Reynolds?

Chapter 13

He took two showers to make sure he'd got the blood off him, his hands so raw by the end his skin felt as though it could peel right off the bone. The events of the night had shaken him, and the thought of what was yet to come shook him further still. The stranger had appeared from nowhere, like a critter crawling out from some long hibernation. But he had come for a reason, and the reason was him. A stranger from his past. Someone who could have filled in the missing parts. But now he was dead, slaughtered like cattle. By whom he did not know, but the stranger's death was a message. A message to him, perhaps.

When he stepped out of the shower, the screen on his cellphone flashed with various missed calls and a text from Amanda telling him she'd heard what happened and asking him to call her. He ignored it, got dressed, swallowed a yellow pill for his headache, then grabbed his keys on his way out of the door again.

The parking lot was mostly empty when he pulled in at Seymour's, and the place had that slow night feel about it as he entered.

Wes glanced up as he came to the bar, busy cleaning down the counters and otherwise surprised to see him at this hour. "What can I get you, Jack?"

"I'm not stopping," he said, spotting Abel Cross sat in his regular spot at the end of the bar, nursing a glass of bourbon.

"Heard you were down at the diner tonight. What happened?"

"Can't talk about it right now."

"Suit yourself."

"What kind of mood is he in tonight?" He shot a look across at Abel, who hadn't noticed him enter.

Wes rolled his eyes. "Mad as a wrongly shot hog."

"Nothing changes then." Jacob followed the bar round to the other side and pulled out a stool to sit.

"Better be a good reason you're disturbing me from my last bracer," said Abel, never lifting an eye to acknowledge his presence.

"Can we talk?"

"I got nothing to say to you."

"I need your help." He flashed a manilla envelope filled with banknotes.

Abel lifted his head now at the sight of it. His back

straightened with interest and his eyes looked as though they had taken on a new color. "What is it?"

"Somewhere private," he said, gesturing for the man to follow him outside.

Abel stood, balancing a roll of tobacco between his lips. "Could use a smoke, anyway."

He followed Abel outside, out of sight of cameras and prying eyes.

"You goin' to tell me what this is about?" Abel said, lighting his smoke.

He showed him the picture of the driver's licence that he took from the dead man's wallet. "I need to find out who this is?"

Abel lifted a brow as he studied the picture. "You blind? His name's right there next to his picture."

"I can see that. But I need to know *who* he is."

"This got anything to do with the guy who got run through tonight?"

"Maybe."

"Well, he's dead now, so what good is that to you?"

"I want to know whatever you can find. Can you do that?"

Abel puffed his smoke and licked his lips. "You know I can."

Jacob handed him the manilla envelope filled with cash. "That's three hundred there. Does that cover it?"

"It's a start," Abel said, pocketing the envelope inside his worn duster jacket. "Gonna cost you at least five, though."

He nodded and sighed. "I'll get you the rest tomorrow."

"I'll see what I can dig up. Ain't no guarantees."

"How long?"

Abel studied the driver's licence once more, then handed it back. "A day or two. Three at most."

"You don't need to keep that?"

"I've seen enough of these in my time to know what's important. Besides, I want nothing to do with a dead man's property."

He nodded, then left him to finish his cigarette and wandered back to his truck. He had one more thing left to do before the curtain fell on this night.

———

"You need to tell them the truth." Amanda held his hand as she sat beside him in his truck, her hair pulled back to reveal the soft angles of her face in the dim cabin light.

They were parked up in the vacant lot of the strip mall just outside of town, the place nothing but a row of abandoned stores and a decaying multiplex left to rot in the shadow of its once gainful days.

He glanced over his shoulder at her as she tightened her grip on his hand, a reminder to him she was right there with him. "I can't," he said, the interior windows all steamed up. "Don't you see how crazy it sounds? How involved that makes me look?"

"It makes you look more guilty not telling the truth. It

always comes out. Now, or at some other point. It always does."

"All the same, they'll think I did it."

"But you didn't."

"People will still think I did, anyway."

"This town has a big mouth and a short memory." Amanda pulled the collar of her jacket high around her neck, the warmth of her breath visible against the bitter air that cut right through to the bones. "Besides, there's nothing to hide?"

"I panicked," he said, the tips of his fingers so numb that he barely noticed the touch of her hand a second time.

"Are you sure you don't know him?"

He looked hard at her and leaned away slightly.

"I'm just asking," she replied, the sudden tension palpable. "The whole thing is just... *strange*."

"That's exactly my point."

"So, who is he?"

"I already told you, I don't know. He turned up at the bar a couple of nights ago. Then last night, after you left, he was outside my apartment. Then he posted a picture through my door."

"A picture?"

Jacob leaned across and reached a hand into the glove compartment, the last place he remembered leaving it. "Shit."

"What?"

"It's not here."

"What are you talking about?"

"The picture. It's not here."

Amanda tilted her head to one side, a nervous look in her eyes. "Not gonna lie, you're starting to weird me out a little."

"It was right here, I swear to God."

"Okay. Maybe you took it out?"

He racked his brain for a thought. "Shit," he said, suddenly remembering exactly where he'd last had it.

"What?"

"I had it on me."

"Where?"

"The diner."

Amanda let out a heavy sigh. "Jacob..." she said, leveling with him now. "Tell me everything's okay with you?"

"How'd you mean?" he said, matching her solemn expression. "Am I crazy? Is that what you're asking me?"

She couldn't bring herself to look at him. "God, no," she said. "I meant the accident. I just thought... I don't think you're crazy."

The long silence that followed threatened to swallow any warmth there had been between them. But Amanda was right. Maybe he was losing his mind after all. "I'm fine," he said.

"But you're not," she said. "You just need to tell the cops the truth."

"No," he said, turning to face her again. "I need to wait."

"Wait for what?"

"Nevermind."

"Tell me..."

"I've got someone looking into it."

"Who?"

"Someone I know. Ex-cop."

"That's not your job."

"I know that, but there's something not right about this. Please, just trust me."

Amanda sat back in her seat, a forced smile on her face as she turned to face the window. "Let's go," she said.

———

Marcus Quinn watched from the darkened corner of the adjacent street as the Ford Bronco pulled away onto the barren highway. Keller in the driving seat. A woman next to him. He waited until they were clear of the strip mall, then stepped out of his Crown Vic and limped down the sodden bank to the river that ran on the other side of the highway. The water was as black as the sky above it, and he tilted his face to the bitter wind that had blown in and carried with it the threat of early snow. He stood and watched the dark ripples of the water as a small animal crept out from the groundcover to drink from the surface, its eyes electric against the murk. A fox or a young coyote. As the animal crept away again, he reached into his coat pocket to feel the cool metal haft of the box cutter in his hand; the blade sharpened to a fine point. Quinn stared down at the knife, the end smeared with the remnants of dried blood, then tossed it into the black water of the river before him. He stood for a moment longer, then climbed back up the filthy bank towards the road where his Crown Vic was parked and reached into his pocket again for his cellphone. He scrolled down the contact list, then pressed the phone to his ear as the familiar voicemail greeted his call.

"Hey, this is Chloe. I can't find my phone right now, so I'll call you back. Unless it's my dad, in which case, I'm still looking for it. Leave a message if you want."

He smiled at the sound of his daughter's voice, the only thing that made him smile at all anymore. "Hi, sweetheart," he said. "Sorry, I know it's been a while now. Anyway, I spoke to your mother last week, and she said she was going to clear out some of your old stuff. Toys and books and whatever else there is, I guess. I told her you wouldn't want that, but you know what your mother's like when she gets an idea in her head, so I'll be taking it all with me. Don't hate her for it, though. Doesn't mean she doesn't love you. She's just doing what she thinks is best. Anyway, I thought you might want to know. Speak to you soon, sweetheart." He ended the call and cast a last look at the darkened landscape. Nothing but blackness for miles, except the naked limbs of birch trees swaying in the wind, the trunks stripped of their birchbark. This was his life now, as cold and desolate as the world around him. He got back in his car and drove.

Chapter 14

"Who's the other woman in our bed?"

He sat up against the headboard and searched for the voice that had woken him. She was sitting in the rocking chair in the corner of the room again; her face hidden in the shadow but her body half-exposed, her nightdress fallen on one side to reveal the silhouette of her bare breast. He knew her name now, but he could not speak it.

"What do you mean?" he said.

She spoke again, and although he could not see her face, he recognized the voice. "Who is she?"

He looked around at the empty spot on the bed beside him. "Who are you talking about?"

"You're sleeping with someone else."

"There's no one here."

"Of course there is."

The sound of his shallow breaths filled the stillness as the woman stood from her chair and stepped forward into the gray light by the window, her left eye partially hanging out of its socket.

He recoiled at the sight of it as the woman stood before him, half-dead in the silence, her arm all twisted as it hung at her side. And then the name came to him and he called out to her. "Alice?"

The woman said nothing, then turned as he laid there and walked out the open door to the hallway. He watched from the bed as she reached the top of the stairs and then descended, a step at a time, until she was gone.

He slid out of the sheets, unsteady on his feet, his head a fog as he followed her, reaching for anything to keep him from stumbling and hitting the floor. He called out to her again, but was met with silence, and as he approached the top of the staircase, he spotted the front door open on its hinges and her half-naked body gliding out into the gray light. He reached for the handrail and staggered down the stairs, calling for her, but his legs were like concrete that couldn't carry him quick enough. As he landed on the bottom step, he lurched for the door, realizing that the house he was standing in was one he did not recognize. He staggered outside and looked out onto a circle of decrepit houses and untended lawns, the driveways empty of cars and people, and the street looked as though it had been abandoned for a hundred years and nature had been back to claim what was rightly hers.

There were no people here.

There was nothing here.

He was alone in this world.

And yet he sensed her presence everywhere.

She was nowhere and everywhere all at once.

He walked the deserted streets, searching, calling for her, his voice lost in a dreamworld in which he was forever forced to wander.

———

Jacob's eyes strained open as he awoke from the depths of some untold oblivion, the sound of water running, but he could not tell where. He could not move, but tried to wiggle his toes like he always did, unsure if this was part of the dream or the real world now, his mind etched with the image of the woman's face, the contours of her cheeks, her breasts. She was a stranger that occupied some deep-rooted part of his psyche. A ghost of untouched memories. And then he remembered what she had said to him in the dream as she left—about the other woman in their bed. *Their* bed.

"Sorry, I didn't mean to wake you."

He turned to see the figure of the slender brunette that graced his doorway, her hair wet and crinkled about her shoulders. He didn't recognize her at first. "You didn't," he said.

Amanda came forward to the foot of the bed, dressed in the same clothes that she had been wearing the night before and carrying a towel to pat her hair dry. "I used your shower. Hope you don't mind."

"Of course not." He felt the weight of his legs return.

"Are you okay?"

"I'm fine." He sat up in the bed and rubbed his face. "I was just getting up."

She smiled and looked about the room for something. "I don't suppose you have a hairdryer?"

He returned her smile with one of his own that told her everything she needed to know.

"I didn't think so." She dried her hair with the towel, then started collecting her things strewn about the floor.

"You going already?" he asked.

Amanda put on her jacket and found her shoes by the door. "It's Saturday," she said, as though the day held some great significance of which he should be aware.

He looked at her, at a loss.

"My mom..." she said.

"Of course," he said. Saturday mornings were when she visited her mother. She had told him as much.

"I'll be free after though," she said, reaching for her necklace on the side table. "If you wanted to do something?"

Jacob rolled out of bed and threw on a clean shirt from the wardrobe. "Why don't I come with you?"

Her eyes held a softness as she glanced up at him, and her head nodded gently at the suggestion. "I'd like that."

She meant it too, he could tell from the whisper of her voice. He cooked her eggs for breakfast, then left with her before the sun was up.

———

"This is Jacob," Amanda said, inviting him to come forward into the room where her mother was sitting in a chair facing the television set.

Patti Wheeler was younger than her gray and tired face suggested, but it was the way that she looked right through him, as though he was nothing more than a shadow on the wall, which surprised him the most. He squatted beside the woman and took her outstretched hand in his, frail beyond its years; her mind in its last fall, clinging to whatever light remained before the darkness set in entirely.

"Are you going to marry my daughter?" said Patti.

"Marry her?" he said, taken aback at the candidness of the question.

"Yes, my Katie," Patti said, "are you going to marry her?" She waited for his answer, and yet her vacancy betrayed any sentiment behind the question.

"No, Mom," Amanda said, sensing the sudden unease that had settled over the room. "He's a friend of mine."

Jacob raised a brow in Amanda's direction, which was met with a heavy sigh and a heave of her shoulders. "A *good* friend," he said, letting go of her mother's hand to stand again.

"Well, I think you'd make a lovely couple," Patti said, reaching across for the illegible note rested on the coffee table beside her. "Here's the list of things I need you to get for me."

Amanda took the note from her mother and slipped it

into her back pocket without so much as a glance. "I'll see what I can do."

They stayed for a while until Patti fell asleep in her chair, her head lolled to one side like a woman who finally looked at peace with the world.

"Some days she's worse than others," Amanda said, standing to leave her mother to rest. "This is a good day."

He followed her out of the room and into the hallway of the nursing home as she raised a hand to her face, trying to wipe the tears away without him seeing. "You said Katie was your sister?"

Amanda turned to face him again and reached for the necklace around her neck and opened the locket hanging from the chain. Inside was a small picture of Amanda and her sister in happier times. "She died five years ago. Mom gets us confused sometimes. Other times, it's like I never existed at all."

He lowered his head, unsure what to say to that. "I'm sorry."

"You get used to it."

"I guess your father doesn't want to see her like this?"

"Yeah," Amanda said, rolling her eyes. "But without me, she has nobody."

He followed her down the hallway, past a line of identical rooms occupied by people much like Patti Wheeler. The place was thick with the smell of stale urine and antiseptic, and the linoleum was the color of faded limes that stuck to the bottom of his boots. This was no place for a human being to see out the last of their days, rotting in the stillness of God's waiting room. They walked back to his truck, where a frost had already settled on the windshield. "What were they like together?"

"My parents?"

He nodded and unlocked the truck.

Amanda smiled to herself. "They had their ways. He loved her," she said, taking a moment to gather herself. "She loved him too, I guess. But I think she stayed with him for me and Katie, mostly. I never understood why. It made for a pretty miserable home in high school. That's why I left home at sixteen. After that, my mom lost all motivation to make a change."

"And your father?"

"He's always been too stubborn to do anything differ-ent. But yeah, they loved each other, in their own way."

Amanda slid into the passenger side as he got in and started the engine. The good mood had all but vanished. "You wanna get a drink?"

"It's ten in the morning."

"I know. But it feels like that kind of day."

"No, I don't want to drink."

"Okay," he said, thumbing the steering wheel.

Amanda stared out of the window at the colorless morning. "I think I just want to go home."

———

He drove her the long way home, but she said nothing about it. On any other day, he was a man who preferred solitude than to keep the company of others. But Amanda was not just anyone, and every second he was with her, he felt alive. He pulled up alongside her apartment on the other side of town and shut off the engine. They sat there in silence for a moment.

Amanda's apartment was much like the rest of them on the street, the white cladding now the color of piss stains around the crumbling paintwork. An old coal grill left to rust in the side alley.

"That's strange..." she said, watching the man who'd just stepped out from her apartment block and crossed the street towards a black Crown Vic parked between two removal trucks. The man was tall, dressed in black jeans and a parka, and walked with a slight limp in his left leg as though weathering an old wound that had never quite healed.

"What is?" he said, following her gaze.

"That man. I saw him yesterday. He came into the bank."

The man got into his car and Jacob made a mental note of the licence plate as the Crown Vic pulled away. "You've never seen him before?"

"Not before yesterday. He said he knew I was on the bus that day and was interested in hearing what I had to say about it."

"Was he a reporter?"

"That was my guess too," she said as she looked him straight in the eye. "Then he asked if I knew you."

He felt his heart miss a beat. "Did he give a name?"

"I never asked. I told him I had no interest in talking about that day to anyone. Then he left."

His chest was palpitating now, his mind turning. "You're sure you've never seen him before?"

"I'm as sure as can be," she said. "But why's he here?"

"I don't know. Maybe he's visiting someone." He cleared his throat, the uncertainty in his voice betraying his theory.

Amanda quit the truck and braced against the cold. "Yeah, maybe."

He reached for the door to step out. "Let me see you inside."

"I'm a big girl, Jacob. I don't need an escort to my front door." She fixed him with a stare as she took out her keys from her purse, her dark hair framing her gentle face that was high-colored from the cold.

He rolled down the window as she closed the door. "I'll call you later."

She smiled, then turned and started for her apartment.

He watched her from the truck until she was inside, then felt the drone of his cellphone in his pocket. The message was from Erin Moss. His new prescription was ready, but she wanted him to call and make an appointment. He closed his cellphone and tossed it to one side. That would have to wait for another day.

Chapter 15

Through the canopy of pitch pines, an otherworldly object dropped into view, its silhouette backlit against the vague glow of the low winter sun.

Dr. Elliot Fraser stood with his head turned to the heavens, watching as the dark object descended through the mountains and into the clearing in which he found himself, its rotors strobing in the fading sunlight, the thrumming of its turbines almost deafening in the heavy air as it approached.

The chopper pitched forward, then backward as it settled to the ground, kicking up a maelstrom of mountain dust and vegetation.

Two faces watched him behind the window as the skids touched down on the landing pad, both dressed in ballistic vests with US Marshal badges pinned to the center. Sat between them was another figure, the face hooded and the body clothed in a red jail boilersuit. Fraser lifted the cellphone to his ear, his voice mostly lost to the roar of the chopper. "He's here."

The marshals alighted with grace, each man reaching back for an arm of the prisoner to hoist him down, his wrists and ankles manacled in chains.

Fraser waited for them to approach, the prisoner hauled along by the marshals as they came to a dead stop in front of the facility. He lifted the hood from the prisoner's face, then took a step back. "Welcome to The Keep."

Eugene Garett squinted against the dull light that remained, his eyes adjusting to his new surroundings. "Where are we?"

"Where we are is not important," Fraser said. "But what we do here *is*."

Garett inhaled sharply, taking in the cold mountain air, then squatted and took up some dirt in his hands and rubbed the rough soil between his palms.

Fraser looked at the marshal bearing the keys on his belt. "You can take the chains off him now."

The marshal shot his counterpart a look whose hand went down to his side, stroking the grip of his service weapon. "We keep them on until he's inside."

"Look around," Fraser said, gesturing to the miles of hardwood forest surrounding them. "He's not going anywhere out here."

The marshal unlocked the hand and ankle chains. Garett massaged the skin around his wrists as the marshal released the heavy shackles.

Fraser led the men through the clearing towards the

facility, nestled in a pocket of the timberline and concealed by a canopy of dense hardwoods in every direction. To the south and west lied mountains, and to the east and north lied yet more.

Garett followed, flanked by the marshals that stood to his rear.

They were greeted by a guard at the front gate shouldering an H&K MP5 who waved them past, then Fraser escorted them across the concourse.

Garett stood with his head turned skyward, watching the tops of the trees sway in the half-light, casting long shadows against the side of the two-storey complex of painted masonry and pre-cast stone.

"I think you're going to like it here," Fraser said.

Garett shuffled forward to join him. "As long as I get a room with this view."

They passed through a series of perimeter gates, each one controlled by unseen eyes as Fraser swiped his identification card across the sensor lock. He guided the prisoner through to the receiving unit, directing him through all the usual booking-in procedures as the marshals took their leave, returning the way they came in.

The receiving unit was small and lined with stations for the intake checks: biometric scanners, full body scanners, a clothes dispensary at the far end of the white-walled corridor. Fraser watched as Garett changed into a loose hospital gown, then waved in the blonde warden stood on the other side of the door, her hair pulled back from her face so tightly it was hard to tell she had any at all.

The blonde warden stepped in, balancing a small injection gun in her palm of her hand.

Fraser took the gun, then glanced up at Garett. "Roll up your sleeve."

"What is that?" Garett said, peering down at the needle suspended by his arm.

"It's a micro-tracker," Fraser said, a vacant look on his face.

"You want to put that in my arm?"

"It's a condition of your stay here."

"Must be a hundred miles of forest in every direction. You said it yourself. I ain't going anywhere."

"We can take you back if you'd prefer?"

Garett paused at that thought, then rolled up the sleeve on his gown and presented his arm like an offering. Fraser rested the barrel of the gun on the underside of Garett's arm, right below the belly of his left bicep, then pulled the trigger. Garett pulled a face as the gun *snapped*, but it was otherwise painless. Just a small, red depression as Fraser lifted the gun again. A spot of blood where the chip had sunken beneath the skin.

Fraser led Garett back down the narrow corridor into an examination room housing an MRI scanner. The patient table pulled out in readiness. "I need you to lie down there," he said.

"What does that thing do?" Garett said, stood with his

back against the wall and looking down at the machine in front of him.

"We run a scan to map your brain," Fraser said, taking a measured tone. "Then we run a simulation of it on our system."

"What kind of simulation?"

"That'll become clear later. It's all part of the research you signed up for." Fraser started for the door and turned back to Garett as he opened it. "I'll be in the next room. Listen to my instructions." He watched from the observation room as Garett eased down onto the table and slid inside the machine, following his instructions on the intercom.

———

He came out of the scanner thirty minutes later. Fraser handed the new inmate a white boilersuit to change into, then they rode the glass elevator to the second-storey. At the top, they stepped out into a large, spherical chamber, the perimeter lined with no less than a hundred single-bed cells built around a central observation tower.

Fraser led Garett down the circular gangway, their feet sticking to the clean white vinyl as they walked past the line of cells, a different face looking back at them from behind the hatches. When they reached the other end, Fraser stepped to one side as a warden came out from one of the side rooms wheeling an inmate strapped into a wheelchair, his limp arms rested across his lap like a monk in prayer. There was nothing behind the inmate's black eyes, and if it wasn't for the gentle rise and fall of his chest, the man could have been as sure as dead.

Garett glanced down at his unblinking counterpart as he went by. "What's the matter with him?"

"He's catatonic," Fraser said, not breaking his stride.

"He came here like that?"

Fraser approached the only cell with the door left open, then turned to look at Garett again. "Of course," he said, then gestured for Garett to enter.

The cell was the same as the others. A simple fold-away bed for sleeping. A desk bolted to the floor. A small television set mounted to the wall, and a separate room with a shower and commode that looked out onto the sweep of mountains.

"I'll let you get settled in. If you need anything, you can use the intercom on the wall over there." Fraser watched Garett as he stood at the perspex window, taking in the surroundings of his new abode.

Garett collapsed onto the bed and just sat there for a moment, relishing in the silence. "I think you're right," he said. "I'll be just fine here."

Fraser pulled the cell door shut and flipped down the hatch. "Good. We start tomorrow."

Chapter 16

He'd almost fallen asleep on the couch by the table light with a book in his hand when he heard the doorbell ring. Jacob rose and went to the door, and on the other side stood the chief, wet to the bone, rain running off the rim of his sodden ball cap like a sluiceway.

"May I come in?" Morales said.

Jacob checked his wristwatch. It was gone midnight, and every hour showed as he studied the chief's weary countenance, his skin drawn and unshaven, his eyes bloodshot and leaden. He let the chief in, then closed the door behind him. "Is this an official visit?"

"Always is in my line of work."

The chief followed him in as he got two cold beers from the refrigerator. "What's this about?"

"We found the other kid from the bus. Name's Troy Baker."

"Why're you telling me?"

"I thought you'd like to know we have his signed confession."

Jacob nodded as he uncapped the bottles of beer and handed one to the chief. "I appreciate you coming out to let me know, but a call would have done the same."

"Well, it's a small town and I like to keep things personal around here." Morales smiled as they clinked beers.

Jacob rubbed his arm and sat to take the weight off his bad leg. "Was there anything else, chief?"

Morales joined him at the table. "Nothing I can comment on right now. I was hoping you might clarify something about the other night for me, though?"

"Okay."

"You said to me you never met this fella before the other night. Am I right?"

Jacob nodded. He knew what was coming next.

The chief gave him a moment longer to respond, then reached a hand into his pocket and produced a slip of folded paper. "Then perhaps you'd care to explain that..."

From the note on the back, he knew what it was without having to open it: the photograph he'd left behind in the diner that night.

Morales unfurled the picture and held it up to his face. "Care to revisit your story?"

———

He told the chief everything he could remember. He had no choice.

"You remember nothing at all?" Morales said, a look of suspicion on his face after he finished.

"That's right."

"Because of this accident of yours?"

"That's right."

"And what interest do you think this man had with you, exactly?"

"Like I said, I don't know."

"This all sounds very convenient, Mr. Keller."

"You can check my medical records. It's all there in black and white."

"Don't worry, I will be." Morales leaned forwards in his chair, taking it all in, his pale face pinched and dulled from the long nights he'd weathered. "Why'd you lie to me?"

"Because I'm still trying to figure it all out myself." He took a slug of beer. "Besides, would you have believed me?"

Morales leaned back but held his stare. "I might have," he said, "but you understand how this looks from my position, don't you?"

He nodded and picked at the corners of the label on his bottle.

"The truth will out," Morales said, reaching into his pocket for a cigarette. He took one from the pack and placed it on his bottom lip. "You should have been straight with me from the start. I could rightfully bring you in for this."

"I know."

"You strike me as an honest man, Mr. Keller. Lord, there's plenty out there that ain't that I have to worry about. Don't give me another reason to come knocking on your door." Morales finished up his beer and stood.

"Can I ask you a question?"

The chief took up his damp coat and ball cap. "Ask all you want. Can't promise I'll answer."

"Do you know who he is?"

"Of course."

"And you know who killed him, don't you?"

"Why'd you ask?"

"Because that's the reason you came here alone. You know I didn't do it."

Morales smiled. "Now, let me ask you a question. You always lived in these parts?"

"No. I was born in Indiana."

"Whereabouts?"

"Connersville."

"Sure, I know it. My brother's out that way. Got a place right there on the Whitewater."

Jacob went to answer, then stalled at the thought. "The what?"

The chief eyed him with an odd expression. "The river..."

He shook his head, drawing a blank.

"You grew up in Connersville and you don't know about the Whitewater?"

Jacob pondered on it. He had nothing. No recollection at all. In fact, he couldn't remember much about the place at all, just mere fragments of his mother and father and their house with a white picket fence. It was the only thing he could remember at all. "I already told you, I have trouble remembering things."

"What about Philadelphia? You have any connections there?"

"No. Why?"

The chief put on his coat and started for the door. "It's probably nothing."

Jacob saw him out, the rain still coming down hard, ricocheting like lead shot off the sidewalk.

Morales braced himself as he stepped outside, the high wind howling through the naked trees. "You call me if anything comes to mind."

"Yes, sir."

The chief turned to go, then stalled. "One more question," he said, turning back to face him again. "Who's the woman in the picture with you?"

Jacob shook his head, feigning ignorance. "I don't remember."

Morales touched the peak of his ball cap as he departed. "I thought you'd say that."

Chapter 17

He woke to the boy tugging violently at his arm. "Get up! Please!"

As he came to, the boy stepped back and looked down at him in his bed, his cheeks wet with tears. It was barely light outside and the lingering of the night was still upon them. "What's going on?"

The boy stood, his body shaking, unable to catch a breath. "My aunt..."

Jacob sprang out of bed and grabbed the boy by the shoulders. "What's happened?"

"I... I can't..." The boy tried to speak, but any words were lost in the terror of whatever he'd just seen.

He had never seen the boy so scared before, and that alone terrified him just the same. "Where is she?"

"Upstairs."

He threw on a shirt and pants and hurried for the door, his bare feet pounding the staircase as he climbed to the second floor. The door to number two was ajar as he approached, but there was no noise coming from inside. As he pushed the door open, it was the smell of damp and mold that hit him first, followed by the acrid taste of chemicals. Ammonia. Burning plastic. Nail polish remover. God knows what else. The place was littered with empty cans and takeout cartons, the carpet tacky underfoot as he stepped inside. It was silent, as though the occupants had long since fled and the dust and dirt had reclaimed this hovel as their own. "Where is she?" he asked the boy.

The boy came behind him, chewing his nails that he'd bitten down to the quick, then pointed to a door down the hallway.

"Wait here," he said.

The boy stood outside, unable to put another foot inside his home. "She won't wake up."

He followed the windowless hallway towards the door the boy had pointed to, blenching at the stench of stale smoke in the air, the carpet damper with every footfall, the sound of a running tap louder as he went. He held a breath as he pushed the bathroom door open, his bare feet treading water up to his ankles.

The boy's aunt was in the bathtub, face up but her head bobbing on the water, eyes open yet unmoving, breasts riding the surface, her hair spread out like long spiders' legs. She did not move. She just floated there as her nose surfaced, then submerged again.

Water had pooled in every corner of the room. On the edge of the bathtub, he spotted a small plastic bag of crushed crystal, a filthy crank pipe next to it, the bowl blackened with pipe wipe.

The water was cold to the touch, and the woman was near dead, if not dead already; her lifeless gaze looking back at him from beneath the surface. He lifted her out of the tub and checked her pulse, faint and thready against her ragged skin. As he glanced back over his shoulder, he saw the boy again, stood there with his own feet in the water, looking back at the wizened body of his aunt laid out on the floor.

She did not blink. She did not move. And from the way he hung his head, the boy knew she might never wake again.

————

"Is he your son?"

Jacob was standing outside the apartment block in the rain as the deputy scrawled something hurriedly into his notebook. He watched the boy, who was being attended to by a paramedic in the back of the ambulance. "No, he's not mine."

The deputy glanced up at him with a furrowed brow. "What's your relation?"

"A friend," he said, quickly realizing that left more questions than answers. "I knew his aunt."

A crowd had gathered from the surrounding streets, rubbernecking at the scene, whispering amongst themselves under the hoods of their raincoats and umbrellas.

"What was her name?" the deputy said.

"Uh..." he looked over the deputy's shoulder and spotted Amanda's car pull up kerbside.

The deputy moved across to his line of sight again. "Sir?"

"Sorry, what was the question?"

"The boy's aunt. What was her name?"

"Her name?"

"Yes, that's what I asked."

He thought on it for a moment and stepped to the side again and watched Amanda hurry over. "I'm not sure."

The deputy fixed him with a stare. "I thought you said you were a friend?"

He didn't know the name of the boy's aunt, and the truth was, he'd never thought to ask. "Excuse me," he said, as he shuffled past the deputy. "I just need a minute."

Amanda came forward, dressed in her work clothes, holding a blazer over her head to cover her hair from the rain as she scurried for shelter underneath the balcony at the side of the building. "I came as soon as I could."

He pulled her to the corner, out of earshot. "It's Ben's aunt."

"Is she dead?"

He shook his head. "I don't know."

"What happened?"

"Looks like she OD'd. Maybe drowned in the bath."

Amanda's eyes went wide. "Jesus. Is there anything I can do?"

As he went to answer, he heard his cellphone ring and

reached into his pocket. "I need to take this," he said, reading the name that appeared on screen.

Amanda nodded and stood watching the rain fall around them.

He answered the call and pressed the cellphone to his ear. "Abel?"

The voice that answered was rough and guttural and made no attempt with pleasantries. "I've got what you asked for."

"When can I meet you?"

"Buy me breakfast and I'll meet you now."

"I can't right now."

"What?"

"I said I can't—"

"I heard what you said, but you also said it was urgent."

"It is."

"Good. There's a cafe on the corner of Main Street. Near the library."

"The one with the window sign that never works?"

"That's the place."

"Can't you just tell me now?"

There was a laugh at the end of the line. "I don't discuss these matters over the phone. Never know who's listening."

"Right. I'll bring my tinfoil hat."

"Joke all you want, Keller. Thirty years on the job taught me otherwise."

"Sure. Hold on a second," Jacob lowered the cellphone

and turned back to Amanda, who was standing with her arms folded across her chest. "I need to ask a favor."

"I was waiting for it," she said, her head tilted to one side slightly and her mouth turned down into the blackest of scowls.

"Something's come up."

Amanda looked around at the scene. "You mean more important than this?"

"It's not like that."

"Why'd you ask me to come here, Jacob?"

He looked her dead in the eye. "Someone needs to stay with Ben. Just until I can sort this out."

"Isn't that *their* job?" she said, pointing at the deputy still stood holding his notebook and waiting.

"He needs someone he knows."

"I get it," she said. "Listen, I like Ben. I really do. But I'm not his mother. And you're definitely not his father."

"Look around. He's got nobody else. Please?"

Amanda stalled, her face softening suddenly as she glanced over at the boy as he stepped down from the ambulance and came towards them. She let out a long sigh. "An hour, that's it."

"That's all I need."

The boy approached silently, his head turned down, eyes fixed on the floor.

He squatted and touched the boy on the shoulder. "Amanda's going to stay with you for a while," he said.

"Where are you going?" the boy said, his eyes red and puffy, but all cried out.

"I won't be long, I promise."

Amanda held out a hand. "Come on," she said, as she took Ben's hand in hers. "You come with me for now."

They shared a look as Amanda led the boy back towards the deputy stood outside the apartment block. All around, people continued to gather as police formed a cordon at the roadside. As he started for his truck, he glanced back over his shoulder to see the boy had done the same. Their eyes met between the bodies of onlookers, the boy but a husk of a child and empty of wonder, his slight frame cutting a fragile silhouette against the harsh realities of the world. He had learned the hard lessons from a young age. Too young for anybody. But behind the eyes lied a hidden strength borne out of his plight. The boy would remember this moment for the rest of his life and would carry with him the weight of it with every waking second. Some days, the pain of his loss would crush him; other days, he would shoulder it until he could find the strength within him to conquer it.

———

He found Abel sat in the window seat of the greasy spoon on the corner of Main Street, a two-minute stroll to Seymour's, which he figured would be the man's next stop on his daily rounds, just in time for first orders.

"Get yourself a coffee," Abel said, lifting the napkin to wipe his mouth, his blue-plate special of eggs, bacon and all the fixings looking about as unappetizing as the man himself at this hour.

Jacob sat opposite and eyed the filth on the floor and the years of grease stains on the walls. "No, I'm fine."

Abel waved the waitress over anyway and she came tottering in heels too high for her talent. "Fix my friend a drink here, sweetheart."

The truth was, there was nothing sweet about her. Not even the winsome smile could muster an urge. Not without the teeth anyway. "Whatcha having?" the waitress said.

"I'll just get a black coffee," he said, reluctant to look at any other offering on the menu.

"What else?"

Abel laid his knife and fork down before he had time to respond. "You heard the man. Just the coffee."

The waitress rolled her eyes and tottered back off to fix his order of a black coffee. Nothing more, nothing less.

"You certainly have a way with women," he said.

Abel flashed a crooked smile and ate his breakfast. "I don't come for the women."

"I can see that," he said, looking down at the man's half-demolished plate. "I thought I was buying breakfast?"

"You are," Abel said. "Didn't say you could eat with me, though."

"You're a real charmer, Abel. Anyone ever told you that?"

"My mother, God rest her soul."

"Listen, I'd love to sit here all day and parley, but I need to be somewhere."

"Hold your damn horses, son. You need to learn the art of conversation."

"Coming from you, that is a fine assessment."

"Well, has anyone ever told you that you're too high-strung? Bad for your blood pressure. I should know."

"Do you have what I need or not?"

Abel reached a hand into his coat pocket and presented a sealed packet on the table.

Jacob looked up as the waitress returned with his coffee, long-faced and in no mood for talking, then went back to her spot at the counter again, counting down the hours which had only just begun. He tore open the packet and removed the contents: a ream of documents spilled out onto the table. On the first page, he noticed the image of the man in the mugshot. It was the stranger, but younger and in better days.

Abel chowed down the rest of his plate of eggs, then pushed it to one side. "That's your friend's rap sheet. I had someone pull it up. I think you'll agree it's rather colorful."

"He wasn't my friend," he said, studying the record and keeping an eye over his shoulder. Abel wasn't wrong. The drifter had lived a felonious life: extortion, racketeering, assault and battery, wire fraud. That was just the start of it, but none of which got him any closer to the reason how he'd once known the man, or why he had bothered to track him down. "Is he connected?"

"Keep reading..." Abel said, preparing a hand-rolled cigarette on the filthy formica table.

Jacob glanced up from the document. "You can't smoke in here."

Able licked the rolling paper and placed the cigarette on top of his ear. "You mind your side of the table, and I'll mind mine."

He passed another eye over the document, then settled it down. "Tell me what I'm looking at?"

Abel cleared the phlegm from the back of his throat and spat a wad on the plate beside him. "Looks like your boy used to keep company with a syndicate in Philly. Irish, of course. Seems like he's been off the radar for a while. Last address was in Altoona, before he got sent to the can."

"What do you know about these people in Philadelphia?"

"Based out of Pennsport. Nasty crowd. Got ties to New York, Boston, Chicago. Heavy hitters. Ice. Junk. Arms trafficking. You name it, they're probably in on it."

He continued scanning the document, turning the pages until he was staring at the image of another man dressed in a leather jacket and slacks, shirt unbuttoned to the chest, and deep-set eyes that hid beneath the brim of a Jeff cap. "Who's this?"

"The man in charge of it all. Jimmy Lynch."

The name seemed both familiar and alien to him all at once—the face, too—as though he were a man he passed in the street most days but never cared to look close enough. He returned the papers to the packet. "Is this it?"

Abel ran the tips of his fingers across his mustache. "What else were you expecting?"

"I don't know what to do with this?"

"That ain't my problem."

"What can you tell me about this Jimmy Lynch?"

Abel smiled his crooked smile again. "Enough to know he's a man you wouldn't want to be inviting into your home at Christmas. Or any other time of year, for that matter."

"Is he still in Philly?"

"He has several legitimate concerns there. Bars. Restaurants. Probably nothing more than fronts for his more lucrative interests."

"You have an address?"

Abel laughed so hard he almost choked. "I think I'm starting to like you, Keller."

"I'm serious."

Abel raised a brow. "Can't help you there, son. But you've got no business with a man like Jimmy Lynch, nor the rocks for it, either."

"I appreciate the concern."

"Your friend's dead for a reason, and if I were a betting man, I know which horse I'd be putting it on."

Jacob pulled out a roll of banknotes and slid it across the table. Three hundred in cash. "Can you get an address or not?"

"I'll see what I can do," Abel said. He didn't bother counting the cash, just pulled two ten-dollar bills from the wrap and pocketed the rest into his coat. "If I could give you some advice... keep your head down. Let sleeping dogs lie. You know what happens if you don't."

Jacob looked at him blankly.

Abel stood and placed the ten-spots on the table. "You get bit," he said, then made for the exit. "Thanks for the breakfast."

Jacob left the coffee on the table without so much as a taste and walked out to his truck. As he stepped out in the cold light, his cellphone rang. "I'm coming back now," he said, but he could hear nothing but the sound of rapid breathing at the other end of the line. "Amanda?"

"He's gone..." she said, her voice faltering over the bad line.

"What did you say?"

"Ben. He just took off!"

"Okay," he said, hurrying for the truck. "I'm on my way."

Chapter 18

He pulled the truck over to a hard stop opposite his apartment block. Amanda was already waiting for him on the sidewalk, stood there like some stray dog in the rain. "What happened?"

Amanda held her mouth to her hand, her throat thick with emotion as she got into the vehicle. "I don't know. One minute, he was right there. And then... he wasn't."

"Weren't you watching him?"

"Of course. I... I turned my back... It was just two minutes."

"He can't have gone far. Have you called the cops?"

She nodded, her hands and chin trembling. "They're searching the area."

He dumped the clutch as he shifted the stick into first and the truck opened up onto the highway, leaving hunks of rubber on the blacktop in its wake. He pulled the visor down to shield his eyes as he drove north. The rain would clear soon, giving way to the low winter sun that had broken through the cloud cover. He pressed his foot to the floor, hard on the gas.

"Where are we going?" Amanda said, her body lurching from side to side.

He took a left at the end of the road and gunned the lights, then picked up the road north-west, past the rusted billboard for the old rail yard. "I think I know where he might be."

They drove the rest of the way in silence. Amanda could not seem to bring herself to look at him. She sat there and hung her head like she had condemned the boy to the gas chamber. But he knew where to find him. The boy had told him of his secret sanctum for times such as these.

He left the truck abandoned by the side of the dirt track and quit the vehicle. Amanda came beside him as he cast an eye down the length of the old rail tracks, which had turned to rust from the years of disuse.

Amanda followed his gaze towards an opening in the chain-link fence which had half-collapsed at the far end of the rail yard. "What are we doing here?"

"Come with me," he said as he started towards it. "Or stay here. I don't much mind."

Amanda followed him as he groped his way through the thick underbrush. She reached for his hand as he helped her through, her skirt flecked with dust and vegetation.

He clambered onto the fence and pressed the broken mesh flat to the ground so they could climb over, and as they clawed their way through the copsewood, they came upon an old sleeping car, blackened and charred from an old fire which had laid waste to the carcass that remained.

He circled the car to steal a look inside, but there was no sign of the boy anywhere through the ruptures. "Wait here," he said as he planted a boot onto the footboard and climbed through the ragged opening in the door.

The car was dark and smelled of dank must and petrichor as he moved through the aisle, the taste of old fires still strong in the air. As he approached the first berth, he could hear movement from inside and he called out into the darkness. "Ben, is that you?" There was no response, and as he slid the door aside, he stepped in and saw the boy laid flat on the lower bunk, his small face lit up from the aperture where a window once belonged. "Can I come in?"

The boy lowered the book he was reading and nodded, but did not speak.

He stepped in and stood beside the bunk and said nothing at all for a long moment, the right words for this moment completely lost to him.

"She's going to die, isn't she?" the boy said, his tender voice more an ache than a whimper.

"All I know is that your aunt's a strong woman."

"She's going to die, I know it. And they're going to take me away."

"No one's taking you away. You can stay with me for as long as you want."

The boy looked up at him, his eyes wider now. "Really?"

"Of course. Until your aunt gets better."

The boy sat up and wiped his eyes dry on the back of his dirty shirt sleeve. "You promise?"

He held out an open hand. "You have my word."

They shook hands like men as the boy stood; the oath sealed at that very moment. "You really think she'll be okay?"

Jacob squatted, then placed his hands square on the boy's tiny shoulders. "Your aunt's had a lot of people in her life give up on her. Don't you be doing the same." They shared a look as though each of them understood one another, and in that moment, he looked upon the boy more a son than a stranger.

"What do you think happens when we die?"

"Don't matter what I think," he said. "All that matters is what you believe."

"I don't know what to believe."

"Well, then you know about as much as the rest of us."

"What about after?"

"After what?"

"Do you think we ever come back?"

"I don't know about that either," he said, "but what I do know is that the only thing you've got to worry about is living the one you've got right now. It's the only thing you can be certain of."

The boy stood in silence.

"None of us deserve to be here. That's what makes it all worth living."

"Okay," the boy said.

"Okay. Now enough with all this talk of dying."

Ben nodded, and as he stood to leave, the boy put his arms around him in an embrace. He wanted to tell the boy the absolute truth: that his aunt was not long for this world; that *hope* was nothing more than a smokescreen behind which lied life's hard facts. A delusion forged by humans to deceive themselves from the truths of the world. But sometimes the truth was best left for another day. After all, it always had a way of making itself known without help from anyone.

———

He waited at the door as the boy wandered back into his bedroom to grab his things. "Just get what you need for now," he said. "We can come back for anything else."

The boy's room was more spartan than his own: an old mattress on the floor, a Steelers poster tacked to a dirty wall, and a few books and manga comics stacked to one side. Ben grabbed a bag from the closet and put in whatever he could find.

"I'll be right out here when you're finished," he said, then left the boy to it and read the text message on his cellphone that had come through. It was from Abel. The message itself was just a single line with an address for the Lynch residence, just like he'd asked. As he looked up again, he saw Amanda come in. "Did you tell them to call off the search?"

Amanda nodded and looked about the room for the boy.

"He's in his room," he said. He took her to one side, out of earshot.

Amanda spoke softly, shaking her head as she stepped over the empty cigarette packets and wine bottles scattered about the floor. "I can't believe she made him live in this," she said, surveying the filthy hovel for a home. "Are you sure you're doing the right thing?"

"He has no one else."

"But there's people he can stay with that do this all the time."

"That's exactly what he doesn't want."

Amanda checked her shoulder to make sure the boy wasn't there. "And if she doesn't pull through... What then?"

"I'll take it a day at a time."

She held his face and turned it towards her. "He's not your responsibility. You're *not* his family."

"I know what I am," he said, then pulled away from her. "And right now, it's the best he's got. Can't you see that?"

Amanda let out a defeated sigh. "Of course I can. I'm just... worried about you."

"You don't need to worry about me."

"That's what all men say."

"Well, I don't know what other men you're worried about, but you forget about me."

"Where did you go earlier?"

He hesitated, then reached into his pocket and withdrew the photograph that the stranger had left for him. The one that the chief had returned to him the previous night.

"Is that... *you?*" she asked, studying the picture.

"Yes."

"And the woman?"

"I'm not sure," he said, then pointed at the face of the stranger on the far right of the image. "But that's the man who died the other night."

Amanda peered up at him with wide eyes. "The one who contacted you?"

He nodded. "His name is Rick Reynolds."

"You remember him?"

He shook his head this time. "But he knew me."

"This picture is old."

"Right. I don't remember anything about it. That's why I need to find out who he is and why he came looking for me."

Amanda's eyes narrowed again as she bit her lip. "I don't like where this is going."

He leaned into her and held her stare. "I need to go to Philadelphia."

"Are you serious?"

"I can't leave this."

"Okay," she said, pulling away from him. "But right now?"

"There's something going on that I need to find out."

"What about Ben?"

"I'll take him with me."

"No, Jacob. You can't do that."

"I just need to speak to somebody, then I'll be back."

"Can't you just call them?"

"It'll be a day, no more."

"You can't take him with you. It's not right."

"Okay," he said, and let out a long breath. "So, why don't you come with me?"

Amanda's jaw went slack at the very suggestion. "No, I can't. I won't."

"Then he has to come with me alone."

She rubbed her face, then gathered herself. "It means this much to you, doesn't it?"

"Yes." There was a long silence, the battle raging inside Amanda's head clear to him.

"I can't believe I'm agreeing to this."

"You'll come?"

"No," she said, waving her forefinger. "I'll watch Ben, but you have to be back tomorrow."

He leaned in to kiss her. "I will be."

"Good, because I don't want him disappearing on me again."

"He won't."

"You're sure about that?"

"I know him."

"And what are you going to tell him, exactly?"

"You leave that to me."

Amanda sighed. "For the record, you're pushing me way out of my comfort zone."

He smiled, then turned to see Ben emerge from his bedroom, a laden bag hoisted over one shoulder. "You get everything you need?"

The boy nodded as he came forward and looked up at Amanda. "I'm sorry I ran off," he said.

Amanda acknowledged the apology with a gentle nod of her own. "It's okay," she said. "Just promise me you won't do it again."

"I won't," the boy said, then started for the door.

Jacob followed close behind and locked the apartment on his way out. "I don't know about you, but I could sure eat a horse right about now."

"Me too," Ben said, with a smile as wide as his small face could muster.

Amanda smiled in return. "Me three."

"Let's go get some food then," he said as they headed for the stairwell. "Ben's choice."

The boy looked back at him, eyes as wide as his smile now. "Really?"

"Sure," he replied.

"Anything?"

"Within reason."

"Burritos?"

"Sure," he said, then looked at Amanda.

Amanda smiled with indifference. "Sounds good

to me."

"Alright. Burritos it is," he said as they took the stairs down and made straight for the truck parked outside. "You know the way?"

Ben nodded empathically as he jumped into the back seat. "I'll navigate."

"Good," he said. "Because I've got something I need to tell you."

Chapter 19

Eugene Garett could hear the call of his name, like an echo chamber in his mind, as he stirred to life. As his eyes struggled open and strained to adjust to the light, the figure of a man took shape before him, a blurred silhouette at first, as though he were seeing the world for the first time. And then a voice called out to him again, clearer now, and less distant than before.

"It's time to go," the voice said.

He picked the sleep from his eye and yawned. His mouth was dry and smelled like rotting waste, and the taste was worse still. He sat up on the edge of his cell bed and glanced up at the figure of Dr. Fraser stood over him. A warden at the cell door. "Go where?"

"Get dressed," Fraser said, his voice but a whisper in the darkness.

He got to his feet, ribs straining through his thin and bloodless skin as he stretched his back. He stood naked, splashed cold water on his face from the faucet, then put on his clothes.

Fraser led the way from the cell, down the maze of silent corridors and gated checkpoints, each one demanding a digital retina scan and key card to pass through. The warden followed a few steps behind, but said nothing.

They crossed through a large, circular vestibule which emerged from a series of similar gated access points and hallways. The nucleus of the facility. Shafts of blue light poured in through the domed glass ceiling high above him, and as he lifted his head towards it, he could see the vault of morning sky that opened up like a heaven to welcome to him. He stood for a long moment as though he were in prayer and let the light touch his face. If there was ever a God, he felt it at this moment.

"Let's keep moving." Fraser came beside him and escorted him towards the gated door directly opposite—the only one of six others that was painted black.

He exhaled, then walked on, like a condemned man on his way to the gallows tree. And it was only then that the thought emerged. "Where is everybody?" he said. It was a genuine question because, despite its size, the facility appeared to be mostly deserted.

Dr. Fraser unlocked the black gate with his key card and waved him through. "We'll be at full capacity soon enough."

They carried on, corridor after corridor, until they

reached an elevator at what he guessed to be the west corner of the facility. They rode the elevator down and stepped out into a glasslike cage with a single door at the other end leading to another room beyond it, where a team of masked figures dressed in white coveralls and hoods stood in greeting. Beyond them, a huge machine took shape, affixed to a black domed shell that was split open like a casket.

As he edged his way further into the glass cage, he realized he was now standing in an observation room, separated from the adjoining clean room by half-inch thick tempered glass from which no noise could escape. Garett stood, arms crossed in front of his body, hands shackled, taking it all in.

"Are you ready to begin?" Dr. Fraser said.

He counted four more hooded figures in the clean room beyond, their backs straight as they waited in a line like an execution squad, their faces covered in surgical masks and goggles. "Begin what?" he said, his voice faltering at the very sight of it all.

"What you came here for..."

"You never said what that was..."

Dr. Fraser smiled as he opened the door at the other end into a smaller decontamination area and gestured for him to enter. "Please step inside."

"I'm not going anywhere until I know what you're going to do to me." He stood his ground as he began to sweat.

Fraser held the door open, his whole manner no more

threatening than that of a child. "I already told you. It's part of our research."

"What's *that* thing for?" he said, pointing to the black domed module in the clean room beyond.

"It's how we map your brain activity. I told you that."

He shook his head back and forth. "I didn't sign up for that."

Dr. Fraser fixed him with a look. "Actually, you did."

"I ain't getting in that thing. You can take me back."

Fraser stood for a long moment, deadpan, then gestured to one of the hooded figures stood behind him. "That's not an option anymore."

He felt a sharp nick on the side of his neck as soon as the words left Fraser's mouth, followed by a feeling of cold liquid coursing through his veins, working its way through his body like a cascade of burning acid. A hand went up to feel the pain as he turned on his heel, and the masked figure behind him stepped back, the empty syringe clasped between gloved fingers.

Before he could react, he felt the room start to turn around him, the figures a distorted assemblage as they encircled him. He stumbled as his legs grew heavy, as though he were walking with an iron shackle made fast to his ankle. He dropped to one knee, his wasted frame buckling as his whole body went stiff, his jaw locked and unmoving as he tried to speak, his tongue so numb that any words he could muster came out as nothing but nonsense. His body hit the floor, and his vision faded in an instant, lost to the very blackness from which he had awoken only minutes earlier.

———

Light.

Bright light flooded his periphery again.

His eyes strained open again, heavy against the force of some unknown weight that wanted to keep them shut.

His body was numb, and yet he could lift a finger, a toe, his tongue.

His head felt like a vacuum of nothingness.

His skin tingled at every pore as the sensation returned.

More light flooded in as he forced his eyes open, blinking through the haze of indistinct shapes that moved around him.

A chair.

A table.

A strange bleeping sound.

Something moved around him. A figure to focus on.

A monitor with flashing lights.

The face of a man took shape as he rolled his neck to one side, followed by a voice, nothing but a murmur at first. "Welcome back."

He focused on the face of the man before him, without blemish and hairless in every respect, the eyes deep-set and unblinking. He knew this face.

He tried to speak, but the words would not form on his tongue.

"You're under heavy sedation," the man said. "You need to rest for now."

As he tried to lift an arm, he felt the tightness on his wrist. As he strained to look down, he saw his hands manacled to the bed he was lying on.

"You need to stay still. It's for your own good."

He tried to speak again, but his jaw was leaden and shapeless.

The figure leaned over him with a half-smile, and only then did he discern the face of the man who had brought him here.

"My name is Dr. Fraser. Do you remember me?"

He said nothing but managed a nod, terrified at whatever hell he had awoken in.

"Good," Fraser said, his eyes electric against the harsh light. "I'm pleased to say the scan was a success."

Chapter 20

Hail fell like lead shot on the windshield as he picked up the highway towards Philadelphia. His plan to square the boy with the promise of burritos had worked. Ben had forgiven his reasons for leaving like he did, but the boy had made him promise he would be back before sundown the day following. He had no intention of being gone any longer, and so he left the boy in Amanda's charge and hit the road after they'd finished their meals.

The sky was the color of gunmetal as he drove the Penna Turnpike east, past mile marker one-sixty-three just past Breezewood. As he pulled into the next gas station to take a leak, a call came through on his cellphone from an unknown number. "Who is it?" he said, lifting the phone to his ear.

A woman's voice crackled on the line. "Jacob, it's Erin."

"Sorry, I didn't recognize the number."

"I know. That's why I'm calling you from it. You've not returned my others."

"I've been meaning to. Just busy."

"When can you come and see me?"

"I don't know. In the next couple of days, maybe."

"I see. Is everything okay?"

"Everything's fine, just a bad time right now."

"In that case, why don't I come by yours later today? I have your new prescription."

"No good, I'm not at home." There was a long pause on the other end as he parked the truck up in a free bay. "Erin?"

"Where are you?" Erin said, but there was something strange in the way she asked it.

"Does that matter?"

"Yes, it does. I said it was important that we get you on new medication as soon as possible. Do you have another address where I can send it to you?" Again, there was something odd in her tone, as if beneath the curiosity lied some furtive purpose.

"Not necessary. I'll call you when I'm back."

"Back from where?"

"Philadelphia."

Another long pause followed before she answered again. "It's important that I see you, Jacob."

"I appreciate your concern. There's just a lot going on for me right now. I'll call you in a few days." He killed the call, stretched his legs, then went to take that leak he'd been busting for. After that, he placed a call to Amanda on the hour like he'd promised. She was none best pleased with his departure, and yet, she understood why it had to be this way. It was in this moment of solitude, surrounded by nothing but the sound of passing traffic and distant birdsong, that the absolute truth came to him. He had been gone barely a few hours and yet he missed her and the boy as though he had been absent for far longer. He could not remember caring for anyone more than the boy and the woman he had met on the bus, but despite his longing for them, there were too many questions that remained unanswered. *Who was he? Where had he come from?* Questions that most men need not concern themselves with. He thought he knew the answer once, but there was still so little he could remember. Perhaps he never would recall such times again, but the stranger had come to him in warning, like a harbinger of some unknown purpose. And now the man was face up on a cold slab for whatever sins he had wreaked on this earth. Sins that, maybe, he had once been wise to. He could feel it. Deep inside him, he knew it to be true. He had once walked this world a different man than the one he was now. That was the man he wanted to find.

———

Marcus Quinn watched from a distance as Jacob Keller quit his truck and made for the entrance to the rest stop. He had tracked the man fifty miles east, and he was certain that Keller was unaware he'd been following him.

He was careful like that. That's why they hired him for this line of work. They wanted a shadow, and he gave them a ghost. It was what he was good at. The only thing he was good at.

Quinn reached for the dial to turn off the radio, then checked the notifications on his cellphone: another news story about an infant drowned in a creek, his naked body left to rot on the side of the bank where the wildlife had made their claim. The third body in as many months. He thought that there were some sick people in this world. That's why he did what he did. Stopping sick people doing sick things to one another so that, maybe one day, there would be a society free of the ravings and deeds of the dangerous. That's what he used to tell himself. But now, he wasn't so sure where the danger lied.

He scrolled through his phone, dialed the first number on top of his call list, and waited for the usual greeting.

"Hey, this is Chloe. I can't find my phone right now, so I'll call you back. Unless it's my dad, in which case, I'm still looking for it. Leave a message if you want."

He never tired of hearing her voice. It was the only thing that made him feel close to her now. "Hi, sweetheart, it's me. I know it's late, but I haven't forgotten. Happy Birthday, sweetheart. Wherever you are, I'm sure you're having a ball. I got you a present. Left it in the usual place. I hope you like it. You know I've never been good with gifts. That was your mother's talent." He paused to collect his thoughts. "Remember that year I got you that Betty Spaghetty doll, but all you cared about was playing with the box it came in? Life as a parent... tragic at times." He fell silent for a long moment and looked out on the stretch of barren road in both directions. "Anyway, I didn't want to end the day without calling. I'll check back in a few days. I miss you." As he ended the call, he picked out Keller in the parking lot as he returned to his truck. He started the engine and followed the Bronco back onto the highway, three cars between them. Soon it would be dark, and from the color of the sky there was more rain to come.

It would be another hundred miles before he stopped again, and a hundred miles more before they reached the outskirts of Philadelphia. It was what they had feared all along: Keller making his way back to places he no longer had any place being. He knew what he had to do. His orders were simple, sacrosanct, and sealed by those with license and whiter collars than his own.

As the Bronco turned down a quiet street lined with maples and pines on either side, he reached for his weapon in the glove compartment: a HKP30L, chambered in nine-millimeter Parabellum, safety off. He hanged back on the adjoining street so as not to give his position away as the Bronco rolled to a stop outside a large house made of glass and stucco. The house itself was set back from a large driveway that was grassed on either side but otherwise designed with the least imagination. A modern, urban blemish amongst the old-world Queen Anne's that occupied this slice of quiet suburbia.

As Quinn switched off the headlights, a text came

through on his phone from the only number he didn't bother saving.

Are you with him?

He typed out a response.

Yes.

A message came back immediately.

Deal with it.

Chapter 21

"Are you okay to wait out here?" Amanda looked at the young boy next to her, his head bowed, lost in a world of his own and not listening. "Ben?"

He looked up at her with eyes that held a distant longing, for he had not yet mastered the ways of hiding his woes. In time, and with enough disappointment, that would come. "What did you say?"

She was standing outside the door to her mother's room, looking in at the shadow of the woman that had once shown her all the love a child could ever need. "She's not very good with strangers."

Ben peered in through the crack in the door, seeing nothing but the back of her mother's head facing the television. "Is that your mom in there?"

She nodded. "Can you wait out here? I won't be long."

Ben managed a smile. "Okay," he said as he sat on the

small wooden bench in the corridor and searched his bag for his book.

"You're not going to run off on me again, are you? You made a promise."

He shook his head and began to read. As he sat there, a boy alone with nothing but stories to escape the bitter truth of the world, she felt something stir inside her. An instinct she did not recognize. Something primal about it, like a dormant intuition blinking to life. It was at that moment that she wanted to show him all the motherly love of which he'd been starved. She wanted to lie and tell him that everything would be fine. But even a child of his tender years could see through such untruths. He was a kid who was not blind to the brutal facts of this existence. He was wise beyond his years, and the world had not been kind to him, but his good sense was born for exactly that reason. The world did not care for reason or quickness of mind, and it treated children with the same cold indifference it treated all else. The only difference between the boy's life and that of her own was that the savagery of existence had found him sooner than it had her.

She left Ben to read on the bench, pushed the door open to her mother's room, then took a step back as a large figure stood from the chair next to where her mother was sitting. She didn't recognize the face of the man looking back at her at first, then reckoned herself some place else when the image finally settled. "Dad?"

Hank Wheeler put a finger to his lips. "She's resting," he said, his head titled down to regard his ailing wife.

"How long have you been here?"

Her father crept round to join her, treading carefully so as not to wake his old lady. "A little while. What are you doing here?"

She looked at him as though he had no right to ask such questions, and he looked at her as uncomfortable as she'd ever seen him. "I'm dropping off some things," she said, lifting the bag of groceries in her hand. "I should ask you the same question?"

He fell silent, unsure how to answer that one without sounding like a plaster saint. He sighed and swallowed whatever pride he had left in him. "You were right."

"Excuse me?"

He kept his voice hushed but said it again, clearer this time. "You were right. I should have listened to you."

"It's not fair," she said. "You can't just decide to come like this. It confuses her. She won't understand."

"I won't do that again."

Amanda rolled her eyes, unconvinced by her father's promise. She'd heard it all before, and not just once. "Sure. Until things get too tough to watch again, right?"

"It's not like that."

She placed the bag of groceries to one side and unpacked them onto the table. "No? Because from where I'm standing, you're here for one of two reasons: to get your fix, or to appease the god who you think gives a shit about your sins." There was a long silence, and when she looked back at her father again, he was crying. She went to him and he turned away from her, wiping his eyes with his handkerchief. She tried again, reaching for his hand to pull it away from his face. "I'm sorry." She wrapped her arms around him like he used to hold her as a little girl. And it was in this moment of tender embrace that she saw her future so clearly. The future where she was no longer just her parents' child. She had always heard that the day would come, but had never imagined it herself. The day where the roles of caregiving reversed forevermore. The difference is that she had to do it alone, and Katie would never be here to share the burden or see the day.

Her father tried to pull himself together but couldn't stem the tears. "No, I'm sorry."

She held her father close, but did not cry with him. All her tears shed long ago. She had only ever seen her father cry twice. The first was when her grandmother had passed. The other was the day when her mother had forgotten that she'd even married the man that she'd shared her life with for the last forty-three years. Those had been painful days for her father. Days that would likely stay with him until he himself was no longer meant for this world.

"I've been a coward," he said, blowing his nose in his handkerchief. "*Still* a coward, I guess."

"You're not a coward."

He held her hand and pulled himself together. "I am what I am, and you know it."

"We all deal with things in different ways." She turned off his stare. The words came off as cheap as they sounded.

176

"Maybe. Except I never dealt with anything at all. I just ran from it."

"I don't think now is the time for a *mea culpa*."

"I've wasted too much of it trying to hide from the inevitable. But I'm done hiding now."

She wanted to believe him, and yet the carousel of disappointment kept her from it. "Don't say things you don't mean."

"I mean it."

She pressed her palms to her ears so as not to hear the empty promises. "Please, don't..."

"I understand you don't trust me with this. But that's what I'm asking for."

"What are you trying to tell me?"

"Spare me the dignity of having to spell it out for you."

"Dignity?" The comment irked her, and she felt her heart race as she looked at her mother, still resting in her chair. "You think there's any dignity sitting in that chair, whiling away the last of your days in front of a screen as your brain rots to nothing?"

Her father pulled her to one side. "Keep your voice down."

"I can't keep second-guessing your motives."

"There are no motives, Amanda. I'm just trying to do what I should have done a long time ago."

"Why now?"

He looked up at her, on the verge of tears again, the hairs on his chin moving with the tremble. "Because any later, and I'm afraid I won't get a chance."

"That's the problem," she said. "It's not about *you*."

"I want to put things right. I made a vow."

"Well, you should've thought about that the first time you quit on her."

"I never quit."

"Call it what you want. It doesn't change the fact."

"I didn't come here to fight with you."

"Maybe not, but you found one anyway."

"I love your mother." He was crying again now.

"And I love her too. Which is why I'm doing your job as well."

"Then let me help."

"You never needed my permission, Dad."

Her father wiped his face dry. "What else do you want me to say?"

"The truth," she said, her face as hard as stone. "Why do you always push me away?"

There was a long silence as her father collected himself. He went to speak, then swallowed the words right back down again, as if doing so bought himself just long enough to come up with some other excuse.

She looked at him; the hardness fading. "Tell me?"

He mumbled something to himself, then stopped again. He looked down at her mother's frail and unmoving hand, then at her withered countenance, which seemed to dwindle and fade with each labored breath, even as she slept. "All the women in my life that I care about, I've lost. Katie. Your mother—"

"I'm still here!"

He nodded. "And there's the truth."

"What is?"

"I can't bear to lose you, too."

They shared a moment of silent tenderness that they hadn't shared in the longest of times. "I'm right here," she said, taking his hand in hers. Nothing more needed to be said. She realized now, even if nothing could give back the lost time, that her father had pushed her away because he was afraid of losing her, too.

As they embraced again, a small voice called out from behind them. Weak and dimming with every word.

"Katie, is that you?"

She went to her mother's side and sat with her. "It's Amanda, Mom."

Her mother studied her face, as if trying to place the image to some moment in time. A second passed, then her mother's face lit up with the smile that she so often yearned for, and behind her eyes was the faintest glow of recognition. "Amanda? Hello, sweetheart."

She tried to stifle the sob but couldn't. The tears came flowing.

"Why are you crying?" her mother said.

"I'm just happy," she said.

Her mother smiled again and looked about the room. "Have you seen that nice man?"

"What man?"

"There was a man here. Right where you're sitting now."

Amanda looked up at her father, who was standing at the back of the room, out of eyeshot.

"I'm still here," he said, coming forward again.

"Oh, I thought you'd gone," her mother said, as if speaking with a stranger she'd only just met. "Come and sit with us."

"I'm not going anywhere, Patti." he said, kneeling beside her.

Her mother nodded and smiled again, but whatever light that Amanda had seen in her mother's eyes just moments before had gone again.

"Have you met my daughter?"

Her father nodded softly. "I have."

"Isn't she beautiful?"

Amanda looked at her father, knowing how hard this moment was for him.

He nodded gently. "She most certainly is. Takes after you, no doubt about it."

"We have two daughters," her mother said, turning to face the man she no longer recognized as the father of her own children. "My other one lives in..."

"New York," Amanda said, finishing the thought.

"New York. Yes."

"I'm sure she's just as beautiful," her father said, a hand to his mouth to hide the shake.

Patti nodded in agreement. "Maybe you'll get to meet her one day, too."

Her father bowed his head. "I hope so."

Amanda stood and left her parents alone to talk like

strangers, and when she opened the door again, Ben glanced up from his book as though she had been gone longer than she really had. "You want to get a beer?"

Ben looked at her through narrowed eyes. "I'm not old enough to drink."

She sighed, then started down the corridor towards the exit. "Too bad. I guess I'll have yours too."

Chapter 22

Jacob sat and waited in his truck until it was dark.

At night, the Lynch residence came alive. Every light in the house was on, and the sound of voices carried on the wind from beyond the gated entrance. Talking. Laughing. But he could not see their faces. There were four, maybe five of them.

As he rolled the window down, he could see a black Escalade being prepped on the drive, headlights on, ready to leave. The house behind it was lit up like some ten-thousand square-foot glass box. More an architectural work of art than a place to call a home.

Five minutes later, he was on the road again, tailing the Escalade from a distance but keeping pace. There was no way of seeing the occupants inside through the smoked windows. He didn't know these roads, but that didn't matter. All he had to do was follow.

Three miles on and the Escalade pulled into the parking lot of a strip mall lined with eateries. He kept close behind and slowed the truck to a crawl as the Escalade parked in a bay outside a small steakhouse. He steered the truck into an empty spot on the row further back, behind a curtain of trees, and watched through the windshield as five bodies got out of the Escalade, their backs to him. The driver stepped out first, followed by a man in a light gray sports coat and black shirt. His face was turned to one side, so all he could see was the back of his balding head. A woman then stepped out from the back of the car, followed by a young girl, highschool age at a guess, and finally a boy, shorter than the girl by a good foot and no older than twelve. They smiled at one another as the man dressed in gray and black placed an arm over the woman and led his family into the steakhouse.

He waited another five minutes before following them in.

The joint was crawling with diners, bodies filled wall-to-wall, eating and talking over the sound of bluegrass and the clinking of wine glasses. The whole town looked as though it had turned out for the night, and the restaurant was loud and electric.

A pretty waitress smiled at him as he entered and scoped the place. There were people everywhere, all of them lost in their own conversations about money, jobs, houses, who was screwing who at work, and who wasn't getting screwed at all. He could hear all of them, and yet none of these people were who he had come for.

As he looked further down, he spotted a small private area with a single table in the far corner of the restaurant, sealed off from the rest of the joint as though reserved for a king to overlook his subjects. He could see the woman now, sitting with her face towards him, her blonde tresses falling about her shoulders and sporting a winsome smile that seemed to come out of nowhere. Opposite her sat the man in the gray sports coat, now hanging on the back of his chair, yet the view was too discreet to get any kind of look at him.

"What can I get you?"

He turned to see the waitress stood next to him, even prettier up close, although her youth was hidden under a layer of makeup and mascara that tried hard to make her look older than she really was. "I don't mind," he said. "Something cold and good for a bad head."

"I can do cold," the waitress said, flipping open a menu. "Would you like to hear the chef's specials?"

"I'm not eating."

The waitress stood, uncomfortable, then closed the menu and set it to one side. "Just something cold then."

"That'll be fine." He found a stool at the bar with a view of the corner table as the waitress went about fetching him his drink, and only then did he notice the sign hanging front and center above the spirit rack: *Lynch's Steakhouse*.

The waitress returned with an ice cold beer and set it down on the mat. He paid in cash and dropped a note into the tip jar.

"New face," she said, cashing up his change. It was more a statement than a question.

He sipped his beer and made nothing of it. "Just passing through."

"I like new faces." She smiled from the corner of her mouth and made eyes at him. "Let me know if you change your mind about food. I'm sure there's something I can find you'd enjoy."

As she moved off, he turned his attention back to the table as a waiter walked over with an ice bucket filled with two unopened bottles. It was then that he saw the man's face, just the side of it, laughing with the waiter who was pouring champagne into their glasses.

He pressed a forefinger to his temple and closed his eyes as that familiar dull ache arrived at the front of his skull, rising like a pressure cooker. He needed something for the pain. Anything to take the edge off. Jacob sipped his beer and leaned across the bar to catch the waitress as she walked past again. "Do you have an aspirin?"

The waitress shrugged. "I'll go check for you," she said, then disappeared into a room at the back of the restaurant.

As she went, he felt a weight on his shoulder and turned to see a thickset man stood behind him, bull-necked and staring at him with black eyes that seemed too small for his face. "Patrick?" he said, the show of teeth telling him it was not a pleasant greeting.

"Excuse me?"

"You've got some nerve showing your face in here like this." The thug came beside him now, muscles tensed as he pulled the stool back from the bar. "Get up."

The top of his beer spilled down the front of his shirt as the thug dragged the stool from underneath him. "You've got the wrong person," he said, trying to placate the beast of a man. But by this point, heads had turned to see what all the fuss was about. He followed the thug's gaze towards the table in the far corner where the man in gray and black got to his feet and looked over, his face twisted into a strange yet knowing grimace at the sight of him. At once, he recognized the man from the file that Abel Cross had procured on his behalf.

Jimmy Lynch was not as tall as appearances let on. He was a small-boned man who walked with a purpose and whose face cut a dangerous shape. As their eyes met across the floor of the restaurant, Lynch's face turned the color of alabaster as he stood there, and it was as though a thousand unspoken words passed between them.

He focused back on the thug, who now had hold of his arm as he lifted him from his stool with little effort. "Listen. You've got me confused with somebody else."

The thug leaned forward and lowered his mouth to his ear, so close now he could smell the stale sweat on him. "Are you carrying?" he said, feeling about his body with a hand.

He pushed the thug's wrist away. "I got nothing."

The thug stepped back and flashed the grip of a pistol holstered to his body concealed under his shirt. "You've gone soft in the head in your old age."

The waitress came trotting back over, laid the box of aspirin down on the bar top. "Here you go," she said, and then a look of disquiet crept across her face as she glanced up to see the thug stood there with him. All three hundred pounds of him. "Is there a problem, Slim?"

"Mind your damn business, Mia," the thug said.

Lynch gestured to a door at the rear of the restaurant, then turned back to his family to excuse himself.

"Let's go," the thug said, pushing him forward as the waitress watched them go.

He walked to the rear of the restaurant, down the walkway, past the faces of patrons at their tables who looked up at him from their meals as he passed. Stony expressions hung on their faces. A stranger in a strange land.

The thug the waitress called Slim elbowed him into the stairwell as he approached the door that Lynch had entered only moments before. They descended the stairs, leading to a small basement office with a desk at one end and a cash safe at the other. Reproduction Rothko's hung on the walls.

Slim marshaled him into a corner, ordered him to spread his arms and legs, then frisked him.

"I'm not Patrick, or whoever you think I am."

Slim stepped back as he took the cellphone from his frisked pocket and placed it inside his own. "We'll get to that," he said, removing his pistol now.

It was then that he felt a crack on the side of his skull as the butt of the thug's pistol pounded his face.

Once.

Twice.

He staggered backwards and the back of his head rapped the corner of the wood-paneled wall as his legs gave way from underneath him, the ceiling above him turning like a suckhole as he glanced up, black and white dots in his periphery as he hit the floor.

As his vision sharpened again, he felt a run of warm blood down the left side of his cheek and he could taste it on his tongue.

"You're right," said Slim, laying the pistol to one side as he hoisted him back to his feet again. "You ain't Patrick."

The thug pulled up a chair and let him fall back into it, then he spotted something square on the floor where he'd fallen: his billfold. It was then that he sensed another figure in the room, watching from the corner.

Jimmy Lynch walked forward into the light, his face marked by the weariness of a man who had grown too old for devilry, and yet there was an air of steadfast menace in the way that he held himself. Lynch patted his face with a napkin, unfastened two buttons on his shirt, and rolled up the sleeves above his forearms. "Is he clean?"

Slim nodded as he squatted to reach the billfold on the floor, then handed it to Lynch, who made no expression. "No weapon. No wire."

"Jacob Keller..." Lynch said, reading from the details on the driver's license as he flipped open the billfold. He came closer now, studying his face through cold and narrowed eyes. "Bible name. It means *the subverter*. In my world, I call that a traitor."

He swallowed dry and held a hand to his head, his palm covered in his own blood as he pulled it away again.

Lynch turned to address Slim now, dabbing his face with the napkin from his table. "Get the man a towel, goddamnit. He's bleeding all over my floor."

Slim nodded, then disappeared up the stairs again, leaving them alone.

Jacob sat in the chair as Jimmy Lynch stood there, silent, until Slim returned with the towel, his head now fit to explode as he pressed the cold compress to his temple.

"You'll have to forgive the loss of words," Lynch said, pulling up a chair opposite him. "This was rather unexpected. But you always did like to make an entrance."

He patted his head with the towel again, which was now turning red from white.

Lynch waited for a response but got none. "Where have you been hiding, Patrick?"

"You don't know me."

Lynch smiled a crooked smile, then pulled opened Jacob's shirt to reveal the tattoo right above his heart. "You're right, I don't." Lynch leaned forward in his chair and pulled open his own shirt to reveal the same ink. "I used to think I did. But not anymore. So, let's skip the small talk and you tell me how you got out?"

He could feel his eyes grow heavy. He blinked through the daze, the left side of his face turning cold and numb. There was nothing left to say that he hadn't said already. All he could think about was how the hell he was going to get out of this bind.

Lynch sighed and got to his feet again. "You've made this real easy for me, Patrick. And for that, I'll give you the courtesy that you never gave me and make sure they do the job quickly. For old times' sake."

A third man entered the room now. He was pale-skinned, with copper hair and a copper beard, and the strength of the color matched his gait. "We're ready," he said, an Irish lilt in the accent.

Jimmy Lynch dabbed his face again with the napkin. "I never much liked violence, anyway. That was always your fine art." He broke into a strange laugh now. "My father used to say that the good Lord works in mysterious ways. I always figured him for a fool. But maybe he was right all along."

He said nothing as Lynch returned to the billfold in his hand and searched through the contents: cash, cards, old sale slips, *the photograph.*

Lynch studied it for a long moment, unblinking, as though the image had stirred something inside him. Then he looked up at him again, eyes as black as coals. "You lost all right to remember her the moment you took her life."

He looked up again, struggling to focus, unsure if he heard that right.

Jimmy reached into his pocket for his zippo, lit it with a strike of his thumb, then held the photograph over the naked flame. It burned, curling at the edges as it turned to ash in his hand. "I want to understand something," he said, looking him dead in the eye. "Why'd you go to all this effort to hide your past, yet keep the one thing on you which ties you to it?"

"I never killed anybody." It was the only thing he could think to say.

Lynch laughed again, but as quickly as it came, it went, replaced with a countenance as cold and dead as the long winter nights. "Forget the sin, forgive the sinner, right? Problem is, I never was the forgiving type, and I'll never forget what you did. But you know the difference between you and me? I've still got time to make peace with God."

"Who's Rick Reynolds?" It slipped out without a thought.

Lynch looked at the faces of the other men in the room. "Rick Reynolds is dead to me," he said. "That's the thing you have in common."

The room fell silent, nothing but the sound of voices and the scraping of chairs from the restaurant.

Lynch squatted so their eyes were level with one another. "You ever see that kid of yours? I always wondered if, one day, he'd come looking for you and ask you why you killed his mother. The whore that she was. I guess we'll never know, 'cause I'm gonna spare you that conversation." Lynch stood again and handed Slim the driver's license and billfold, then started for the stairwell. "Get someone to check the address. See what he's hiding there. Then burn it all."

Jimmy Lynch never looked back again, and as he left, all Jacob could hear was the pulsing in his ears. There was barely a second to process the thought when Slim and the russet-haired Irishman hoisted him to his feet again.

"Let's go," said Slim.

They escorted him out through the back exit to the parking lot, towards a waiting van sat idle with the engine running.

The waitress from the bar was leaning against the wall as he came out, a trail of smoke escaping the side of her mouth. "Where are you taking him?" she said, stubbing out the last of her cigarette as she came over, studying his bloody face. "Jesus, you worked him good."

"Get back to work," Slim said, turning on her, dead behind the eyes. "You saw nothin'."

She shuffled back inside. No questions asked.

Slim opened the rear doors to the van and pushed him forward. "Get in."

He stalled. To the right of him was a ten-foot chain-link fence. To his left, the parking lot at the front of the restaurant. He figured he could outrun Slim, who didn't look like much of an athlete. But the Irishman, concussed or not, wouldn't be so easy.

"Don't make this harder than it needs to be," said the Irishman, gesturing for him to get into the back of the van as he stroked the grip of the pistol that was now hanging from his hand.

He nodded, eyed the darkness of the van as he approached. All he could hear was the muted sound of music and revelry from the restaurant. He stepped closer still and felt his body tense as he placed a foot on the rear of the van. Slim was next to him now, smiling behind the open door.

As he lifted his other foot off the ground, he paused, turned, planted the sole of his boot into the metal door and sent it swinging sideways into Slim's face.

The big man went down hard, his nose split open as he hit the dirt. The sound of metal on bone crunching through the silence.

Then the Irishman was on him, driving him backwards as he came in swinging, each blow landing with such precision that he felt every gasp of air knocked from his lungs.

He dropped to his knees, felt the cool pistol barrel against the back of his skull as he went to stand again.

"Just give me one more reason..." the Irishman said.

Jacob raised a hand in surrender as Slim scrambled to his feet, blood spilling from his lacerated septum. His nose was so bent and twisted it no longer looked like one at all.

Slim reached out a hand to steady himself on the side of the van. "I can't see shit!"

"Get in the front," said the Irishman.

The last thing he heard was the crack of the pistol against his skull again.

Then blackness.

Chapter 23

He woke again in darkness, devoid of time and space. A hard rumble beneath him. The sound of an engine turning. Tires moving over rough ground. His body pitching from side to side in the blackness. It took him a second to remember where he was. His brain a half second behind everything else.

He was lying in the back of the van, his hands and legs bound by some unseen shackles as Lynch's men drove him to whatever godforsaken place they could find to do their deed. But he wasn't dead. He felt sick to his stomach, and the darkness was stifling, but he was nowhere near dead. Not yet.

The muffled voices of the two men came from the front cab, talking through the ways they would dispose of his body after they'd put a bullet in his head. Bury him. Burn him. Maybe both, to be sure. They laughed, then talked women, whiskey and wasting. From the way they spoke, all of this was nothing more than a pastime for these men.

They drove what he'd guessed was another ten minutes before he felt the van slow to a stop. The stillness that followed was even more disturbing than the motion. This was the spot they had chosen. He knew not why, but this was the place that he would die tonight.

He heard the crunch of footsteps treading dirt, a breezy whistle as they went, making their way to the rear of the van. Then the doors opened, the veil of black lifting slightly as the faces of his killers darkened against the pale and colorless moon that hung about the pitch black sky behind them.

They reached in, grabbed his tethered arms, and dragged his body to the dirt. Neither man said a word as they cut the rope that bound his limbs.

He squinted, letting his eyes adjust to the half-light. He was in a field somewhere, more waste than wild. The faint mirage of a building off in the distance. A barn perhaps. Maybe an old, rundown slaughterhouse. He couldn't tell. And as he looked about himself, more structures emerged from the surrounding earth. Steel beams rising like spires. Cinder blocks scattered about a network of trenches that vanished into the shadow beyond. And then he realized the field was not a field at all, but a vast construction site with half-erected buildings that stretched as far as the light carried.

The two men hauled him before a trench that would

soon become his grave, and he looked up at the stars that turned in the black and timeless void above him.

"Here we are, Patrick," Slim said, his tan monk straps covered in dirt and his white button-down all bloody down the front, "or whatever name you go by these days."

His first thought was to run, but he'd be running headlong into a darkness unknown and against men who wanted nothing more than for him to try. All around him was formwork, and beyond that, the flat open land into nothingness. He stuttered a sentence, his mouth dry and thirsty. "I'm not who you think I am."

"You keep saying that," Slim said, but it came out all garbled from his busted nose. "You should have stayed gone."

"Listen to me!" His voice carried long on the wind but was lost to the barren waste on which he found himself. "He came to me."

The Irishman approach, head tilted to one side with interest. "Who?"

"Rick Reynolds."

The Irishman's jaw tightened at the mention of the name again. "Where is he?"

"Lying on a slab right now, I'd imagine."

"You killed him?"

"No."

Slim grabbed him by the scruff of his shirt and leaned into him. "Then someone else saved us a job."

"If it wasn't you, then who was it?" said the Irishman, looking hard at him.

"Man was no stranger to foes," Slim added, "but we all knew that."

He shook his head. "That's the thing, *I don't*. I don't remember any of it."

Slim pushed him back and looked upon him like some pathetic excuse for a man, eyes shifting in the gloom. "What happened to you, Patrick? You ain't the man I used to know. The man feared by many."

He lifted his head and wiped the sweat pouring from his brow. "I don't know any *Patrick*. My name is Jacob Keller."

Slim squinted and tapped the loaded pistol against the side of his leg, believing none of it and sick of hearing it. "I guess I'd want to forget the past ten years if I were you, too."

"It's the truth."

Slim looked at the Irishman, then back at him again. "Tell us one thing," he said. "How did you get out?"

He shook his head and drew a blank expression. "Out of what?"

Slim spat to one side. "The joint. What else?"

Jacob stood speechless.

The Irishman came forward now, baring his teeth like some rabid dog. "Should've put a needle in your arm for what you did."

He felt his skin chill as he glanced up again, and the hairs on the back of his neck stood on end at the sudden sight of her. The once nameless woman of his dreams. She was there, right behind the looming figures of his killers, emerging from the darkness like some creeping wraith, a forefinger pressed to her lips as she crept forward across the filthy waste towards him. Until now, she had only ever haunted his dreams, never his reality.

Slim leveled the barrel of the pistol at a spot just above his eyes. "Death's been waiting a long time for you, Patrick. I'm just the middleman."

He couldn't think. He couldn't breathe. All he could feel was every second of his life drifting into the blackness beyond as Slim's words repeated like some prophecy unfolding. And all he could do was stand like some shackled convict at the edge of a hollow dirt trench that would be his resting place. And when all was said and done, his body would be buried under a sea of concrete, never to be found again.

The Irishman jeered as Slim took another step closer and held the gun to his head. "She deserved better than you."

From the blackness came the sound of footfalls across the brushwood as the nameless woman crept forward, raising a gun of her own and taking aim at the back of the Irishman's head. It was only then that his killers stopped their jeering as the footfalls cut through the stillness.

The muzzle flash came with the *crack* of the round. The Irishman fell headlong to the ground before he knew any different, his eyes unblinking as his corpse rebounded in a billow of dust, then settled like some mannequin in the dirt.

Jacob's eyes met Slim's as he looked up again. Slim

turned on his heel, as fast as his heavy bulk could carry him, and let off a round into the blind blackness but found nothing but empty air.

Slim stood, eyes darting back and forth as he scanned the darkness for movement, his gun sweeping the land about him as another round went up and he staggered back onto one foot.

Another round followed.

Then another.

And another.

Each one punching their way through Slim's chest before the fifth one put him down, next to the body of the Irishman, where both men lay like dead dogs next to one another.

The silence that followed was as quick and violent as the gunfire it replaced, and when he lowered his hands from his face, he saw the ghostly image again. But this time it was not the woman at all, but a man. A man whose face appeared familiar to him. He could not place it at first, not until he came closer, limping on his left leg. It was the stranger he had seen outside Amanda's apartment block. Unmistakable, even on the darkest of nights.

The man squatted next to the Irishman's body and searched his pockets. "Hold still," he said, then stood again and came forward with the keys and loosened the shackles on his ankles.

As Jacob shook off the fetters, he glanced up to see the stranger walking back into the shadows.

After a few steps, the man turned again, his voice as

dead as the men he had slain. All he said was, "Come with me."

Chapter 24

The cruiser slewed to a stop as the tires hit ice and then the curb. Chief Morales shut off the engine and sat for a moment, watching the dull yellow light that framed the window of the ground-floor apartment. The drapes were pulled shut, but someone was home.

The first night of snow had turned to a filthy sleet and then to rain. He studied the dark and sodden street from behind the wheel, waiting for a break in the fall.

Outside the apartment was a black minivan parked across the curb strip, the driver's door left ajar. Whoever had been driving had decamped in a hurry.

Morales threw on his ball cap and watched the rainfall from the cruiser. The ball cap had once been a flawless tan when it was new, but the years of sweat and dirt had spoiled its color and robbed it of its shape. It would be his third visit to this apartment in as many weeks, but he'd stopped counting the days when they started in darkness and ended much the same. He couldn't remember a time when he'd had to pay so much attention to one man before, and he got to thinking that Jacob Keller was some kind of ill-fated menace in his town. Just like the shiver of cold nights heralded the coming winter, Keller had been no less a harbinger of misfortune since he'd laid eyes on him. Trouble seemed to shadow him and linger everywhere he walked. But this time, he wasn't here for Keller. He was here for the young boy in his care.

As the uncounted seconds passed, Morales rehearsed the speech again in his head that he'd played out for the past hour. He was here for a reason, and the reason alone made him shudder. He'd never had to break such news to a child before, the consequence of which would forever strip the boy of all his unworldliness. He was here to deliver certain news. News where any words that follow go unheard. He could feel the palms of his hands sweat as he checked himself in the rearview mirror and recited his line aloud. "I'm sorry to tell you that your aunt died earlier tonight..." No matter which way he said it, it never felt right. He considered himself a thief. The man who would forever plunder a child of his innocence, for today the boy would stop being a child at all and see the world for what it really was. Both its beauty and its ugliness. A world that cared for nobody, however tender your years. He was a thief. That was his burden to bear. And as much as he would have wished for it, he trusted not a single soul to do the job for him.

He checked the time on his watch and breathed a

heavy sigh at the late hour. This would be his last call of the day before he turned in for another night. He knew the house would be silent when he got home. His wife would be in bed, just like she'd told him. A tepid plate waiting for him to warm up in the microwave. He'd eat alone, then go to bed, and pray he'd wake up in a world that differed from the one he'd seen today. He prayed for that most nights, although God did not seem to listen.

As he quit the cruiser, he hurried for the sidewalk and turned his face from the driving rain that lashed down in the crosswind. He scurried past the minivan with its door open. Didn't bother to look inside as he made haste towards the apartment. He wiped the rain from the side of his sunken cheek and lifted a hand to knock on the door. To his surprise, the door eased open on its hinges as he rapped it with a knuckle. He stepped in, treading glass into the carpet from a broken vase which had fallen and shattered into tiny pieces across the dark hallway.

There was an uncanny silence about the apartment. He did not call out or signal his arrival. He felt his left hand drop to his belt and unfasten the thumb break on his holster, instinct kicking in. Something was not right about this scene. As he inched slowly down the hallway, he heard the drone of a television set playing somewhere, growing louder with every forward step.

As he rounded the corner into the living room, his eyes fell first upon the boy, sat still and cross-legged on the couch in the dark, his small face obscured in the faint blue light of the television, yet the whites of his eyes seemed to flash as he turned to look back at him.

Next to the boy was a woman. Her body was stiff, her faced dimmed, yet there was enough for him to recognize her as the same woman from the bus. The woman speaking with Keller when he arrived that morning.

As the light fell down their faces, he noted the black cloth covering each of their mouths. Then the rope lashed about their wrists. Neither woman nor child could say a word as he came in, his shadow trailing off the wall as he edged forward into the room. His fingers closed tightly around the grip of his service weapon as he held the boy's stare, then turned to see the shape of a man stood at the far end of the room.

He swallowed a breath and his hand froze as he lifted the gun just slightly from its holster, benumbed at the very sight of death itself, stood watching him from the darkened corner.

A voice came from the shadows. "Walk out of here and don't look back."

In that moment, he felt the full weight of his body through his knees, as though it were some burdensome shackle from which he could not flee. Then he felt one leg move as his leaden boot edged backwards, towards the hallway from which he came, but his gaze remained fixed to the shadowed man before him. One boot followed the other as he inched back further towards his freedom. His hand never left the gun. There was no time for thought, but there was a second where all he could hear was his wife's voice calling to him like some ushering angel telling him to come home. He should have gone home already. He should never have come here tonight. It was always his worst fear, that there would be a tomorrow where his wife would wake to an empty spot in her bed where her husband should be. But it didn't need to be that way. All he had to do was turn and leave and forget he ever stepped foot in this grim place on the grimmest of nights. He would wake tomorrow next to his wife, and the days after that.

He retraced his steps in slow and labored motions. His hand remained fastened to the grip of his service pistol, fused in its numbness. Only his legs moved.

At the door, he turned and met with the wild eyes of the child and the woman again, their faces beseeching in the muted light.

The woman's eyes went wide, as if trying to communicate some terrible secret.

That's when he heard the *click* of a hammer cocking.

He hadn't seen the second man.

Hadn't heard him coming from behind.

Never felt the bullet tear through his skull.

Chapter 25

Jacob followed the man out of the wasteland, through the length of fence where it had been cut, towards the Crown Vic parked across the road. Wherever they were, the street was deserted at this hour. No whispers of life anywhere, save the gentle baying of a coyote somewhere, and the shadows of bats in flight.

"Where are we going?" he said.

The man who had saved his life limped to the car, its sidelights flashing his arrival as it unlocked. "I'll explain on the way," the man said, holstering his weapon as he opened the driver's door.

"I ain't going anywhere."

The man looked at him. "From where I'm standing, I don't think you're in a position to negotiate."

The man was right, and if Lynch's plan had played out as expected, his body would be buried under a pile of dirt and concrete by now.

"Look around," the man said, gazing upon the silent barrenness that surrounded them. "You're ten miles from anywhere with a pulse. You can come with me and take your chances, or I'd say you got about twenty minutes before another crew turns up here and realizes you're not where you're supposed to be. Choice is yours."

He was alive, and that fact alone was enough to trust the man that had saved him from the certain alternative. He walked around to the passenger side and opened the door.

"I believe this belongs to you..." The man reached into his pocket and tossed something small and square over the hood of the car.

He caught it with both hands, then looked down at the cellphone in his hand. The screen was cracked and soiled but was otherwise working save for the lack of reception.

The man stooped to get in the car and keyed the engine, then left it idling for a second.

Jacob looked about the empty highway illuminated in the dull shaft of headlights. The air was icy and a low mist clung to the night like a stray and wandering curtain. He thought that one day this place would be something. A place of dwellings and abodes where kith and kin would call a home and the generations thereafter. Another stretch of unbroken land lost to the will of man. It would be all of those, but it would not be the place he'd die today.

———

They drove for ten miles without seeing another vehicle. The man did not speak, and he sat in equal silence alone with his thoughts, staring out of the window at the passing fields and highway that had taken on new color with the first hope of daylight.

As they passed a dying cornfield where the stalks stood like brown wraiths against the smattering of light snow, he tilted his head to the man behind the wheel and studied his face again. "I saw you the other day."

The driver kept his focus on the road. "That so?"

"What were you doing in her apartment?"

The driver drank from a bottle of water in the center console, looked across his shoulder at him, then offered him the dregs that remained. "You were there?"

He shook his head to decline the water. "I was there."

"Then you'll know she wasn't in."

"I do. She was with me. What do you want with Amanda?"

"I needed to know what she knew about you."

"Why are you following me?"

The driver shot him another sideways glance. "Because that's what they pay me to do."

A long silence followed. Jacob sat up, his mind turning through a thousand reasons and coming up blank. "Who are *they*?" he said. "And who are *you*, for that matter?"

The moment lingered without response. The man drove on, past an old farmhouse that collapsed on one side. As they came to a crossroads, the driver eased off the gas and let the car roll to a stop. "The people I work for have a vested interest in your welfare."

The reply caught him off guard. It had not been what he was expecting. "What are you talking about?"

"Everything else is above my pay grade. I just do what I'm told to do."

"Which is what, exactly?"

The driver opened the glove compartment and retrieved the folded copy of the *Post-Gazette* from inside. The date on the front was from three weeks prior. Someone had circled the headline in black marker next to the picture of his face, and the lede labeled him the "Brave Man of New Brunswick".

He skimmed over the article. "As far as I know, journalists don't go around killing folk."

"I'm not a journalist, but you'd be surprised what lengths some would go to."

"Then I'll ask again: what do you want with me?"

"I'm here because of what happened on that bus. You've become quite the noble citizen."

"You're not answering my question."

The driver inhaled sharply and rolled his window down to take in the cool air. "Part of my job is to monitor your whereabouts. What you're doing. Where you're going. You get the picture."

"On whose authority?"

"The Commonwealth of Pennsylvania. And higher than that, I imagine."

"What?"

"You heard right."

Jacob steeled himself. "Tell me your name or I'll walk right now."

The driver looked on, deadpan. "In case this wasn't obvious to you, this isn't a brokering deal."

He reached for the handle and opened the door to leave. "You said whoever you work for wants me alive?"

"I said they had an interest in your welfare."

Jacob smiled. "Then you ain't gonna shoot me." As he went to leave, he felt a hard pull on his arm and turned to see the driver had hold of him with one hand.

"Quinn," the stranger said. "My name's Quinn."

He held the driver's stare for a moment longer, then sat back in his seat. "Where are you taking me?"

As Quinn returned both hands to the wheel, he glanced up in the rearview. "To someone who can tell you more than I can."

"How did you track me here?"

"It's what I do."

"You're lying. You couldn't have known I was in the back of that van."

A small smile settled on Quinn's face. "You have a scar on the inside of your left arm," he said, eyes on the road again as he drove on.

Jacob turned his arm over and studied the small white mark on the skin just below the belly of his bicep, right where the driver had said. A perfect cicatrix, barely visible unless you looked close enough.

"That's from a subdermal implant which contains a unique integrated circuit RFID," said Quinn, handing him his cellphone.

On screen was a composite map layered with various readouts and information. Every street in the nearby vicinity plotted out just as they appeared on the ground. On the map was another tiny blip, moving fast as he tracked it with his finger.

"It's a tracking device," Quinn continued.

Jacob ran a finger across the scar site, then looked back down at the blip on the cellphone screen. It was *him*, and suddenly everything made sense. It was how Quinn had traced him here. There was no other explanation for it. But that fact alone raised more questions than answers.

Quinn spat out of the window and loaded a fresh stick of gum into his mouth. "Your next question is why you have a tracking device in your arm. Truth is, you're not who you think you are. You're not Jacob Keller. Because he never existed to begin with."

He could feel his heart drumming through his chest, his palms sweating. Then he noted the man's gun holstered at his hip. It was within reach, but it would not be easy to relieve the weapon from its thumb break. "Who the fuck are you?"

Quinn looked at him again, his voice devoid of all emotion. "I'm the reason you're still breathing. The real question is... *who are you?*"

"How many other people have you killed?"

"As many as we needed to protect your identity."

Jacob let that sink in. "It was you..." he said, the realization dawning on him. "At the diner. You killed that man." He stole another glance at Quinn's holstered pistol, then met the man's eyes as he looked up again and exchanged a knowing glance.

They both went for the gun at the same time.

Quinn's right hand dropped from the wheel at once, but his left was not quick enough to counter Jacob's fist as it rounded on his chin, forcing the car to a hard left. Tires spun on the blacktop as it swerved from the road.

Jacob let another fist fly. Then another. And another still. Each one more brutal than the last and turning the man's face bloody, giving him enough time to loosen the thumb break and draw the HKP30L from its holster.

Tires slewed on the road slush as it slid to a dead stop and mounted the curb.

Quinn pressed a hand to his face to wipe the blood from his nose, then lowered it again to see the barrel of his own gun trained on him. "Go on," he said. "Do it."

Jacob stalled as he looked down at the image of Quinn's beaten face beyond the front sight, unable to finish the job.

The sound of a ringing phone broke the definite silence that followed, and any prior thought of shooting the man was suddenly gone.

The phone rang out as Quinn wiped yet more blood that was forming around the top of his lip now. "I need to get that."

He kept the weapon on him. His hand was steady, as though the feel of the grip and the weight of it calmed him. "Who is it?"

"You want answers?" said Quinn. "Then let me take this call."

He considered it, realizing he was less in control of this situation than he thought. If Quinn had been tracking him, then someone else could easily be tracking Quinn in return. "Okay, answer it."

Quinn reached for his cellphone. "I'm here," he said, pressing it to his ear. "Yes, he's right here with me. I'm passing you over."

As Quinn handed him the cellphone again, Jacob paused and took stock of the situation, a sense of unease settling over him. The answer to all his questions was at the other end of that call. He took the cellphone and held it to his ear, leaving his other hand to work the weapon. "Yeah?"

There was nothing at first, then a voice came through. A woman's voice. "Jacob?"

He did not recognize the voice at first. "Who is this?"

"You know who it is."

It took him another moment, but he did. It was the southern lilt in her accent that made him sit up. "Erin?"

"I know this must come as a shock."

"What the hell is going on here?"

"I appreciate you're confused right now, but it's a little hard to explain over the phone. Can we meet?"

He looked at Quinn, who was still nursing his bloody face. "Who is *we*?"

"I'll explain everything when you're here," said Erin. "You have a choice to make now, Jacob. But if you truly want to know who you are, you're going to have to trust me."

"I already trusted you."

There was a long pause. Nothing else to say.

"Please pass the phone back to Mr. Quinn now."

He passed the phone back as asked, sat back in his seat, and set the pistol down on his lap. His body was numb, his head pounding as he sat there.

"Okay," said Quinn, speaking into the phone again. "We're on our way."

———

They turned off at the next exit, taking the highway north. The curtain of black lifting as a new day dawned.

"Where are we going?" he said, the pistol still rested on his lap.

Quinn kept his eyes fixed ahead, nothing but open road for miles. "It's not far now."

Jacob gazed out at the sight of endless fields, each one more barren than the last. "Who is she?"

"Who?"

"Erin Moss. If that's even her name?"

"Only name I know her by."

"You work for her?"

"She's the one you should be asking."

"I'm asking you."

Quinn sighed, but a calm and collected countenance masked his vexation. "We work for the same people."

"But you answer to her?"

"For now."

"You served?"

"In a past life. Got out a long time ago now."

"Where?"

"Maghreb. Iraq twice. Serbia once."

"Why'd you leave?"

"Personal reasons."

He sensed something in Quinn's voice. This was a man who knew pain in his life. A man who lived in the shadow of suffering. "You married?"

"Why all the questions?"

"I like to know who I'm dealing with."

Quinn relented with a nod. "I'm married, but I'm not sure what that word means anymore." His tone was as dead as the land about them. "We don't talk much."

"Kids?"

Quinn took his time to answer. "A daughter," he said, a crack in his voice at the mention of her.

Jacob let the silence linger for a long while, the air thick with unspoken sentiment known only to the man to whom they belonged. Another moment passed, then Quinn reached a hand into the center console and withdrew a hip flask kept hidden for such times. He took a long swill as though it were a private custom, then passed the flask over. He took the flask and a swig of his own and let the warm liquor hit the back of his throat.

"You're luckier than most," said Quinn.

"How so?"

"Not everyone gets a second chance like you did."

He didn't know what to say, and if he was honest with himself, there was a part of him that didn't want to press the point any further. "You said I'm not who I think I am?"

Quinn nodded, then turned his eye to the road again. "Erin should be the one to tell you, but I have a feeling you ain't gonna like the answer to that question."

"None of this is making any sense."

"Of course it doesn't. You were never supposed to be here. I was never supposed to be here, either."

He glanced back out of the window, his mind trying to piece it all together and getting nowhere fast. "You ever feel like none of this is real?"

"How'd you mean?"

"Out there. All that space. Everything you see and believe to be true."

"Trust me," said Quinn, reaching for the hip flask again. "You don't even have to look that far. Reality is just another misplaced state of mind."

"If that's the case, then how am I any luckier than you?"

Quinn smirked at the notion. "We all have our

demons. The difference between you and me is that you can't remember them."

He sat there with the pistol in his lap. The skeleton grip. Black. Oily. Evil. "What kind of demons?"

They exchanged another look, then Quinn eyed the road ahead once more. "You'll find out soon enough."

Chapter 26

It was light by the time they reached the access road off PA 45, and all around razor wire glistened in the low sun as Quinn wheeled the Crown Vic slowly towards the perimeter fence. Beyond that lied nothing but the shapes of mountains that swelled into a colorless sky.

A white Chevy Tahoe parked at the side of an entrance gate came into view as they approached, and a man stepped out to greet them as they crawled to a stop, his eyes hidden behind dark sunglasses. The man stopped a few yards in front of the vehicle, spoke something into the radio clipped to his vest, then approached the driver's side with one hand rested on the grip of his sidearm strapped to his thigh.

Jacob sat up in his seat as Quinn reached a hand into the center console and pulled out some folded papers. "What is this place?"

Quinn didn't answer, just rolled down his window

and breathed in the cold air and smiled as the guard edged slowly forward.

"This is private property," said the guard, his mustache as white as his shirt. From the emblem on his jacket, this was not a military man, but a private contractor and otherwise equipped to look the part.

Quinn presented the folded papers.

The guard studied them for a moment, then handed the papers back. "How's the weather today?"

"Better than yesterday," Quinn said, as though he had rehearsed the line a hundred times or more. "But I'm looking forward to tomorrow."

The guard nodded as though some secret language had passed between the two men, then signaled for them to pass through.

They drove on, through the bends in the trees, until the access road behind vanished into the mountains themselves. Small plots of land lay scattered between a copse of hardwoods occupied by moss-ridden Quonset huts that had long since fallen to the weather and lost their shelter and shape. And beyond the huts lied an old water tower next to the remnants of a collapsed barn.

Jacob glanced up at the razed land ahead and the rubble that remained from bygone days. "People used to live here?"

"A long time ago," Quinn said.

"What happened?"

"There was a village here once. The federal government seized the land under eminent domain at the start of the Cold War. They cleaned house and laid waste to everything to build an ordnance depot here. What you're looking at is what remains of it all."

He looked about at the desolation as the road came to a sudden end, and Quinn stopped the car. "There's nothing left..."

Quinn shut off the engine and pointed to a small structure hidden amongst the brushwood: a small steel door leading to nowhere. "That's because everything's below ground."

As he looked again, he noticed the steel door open on its hinges and the figures of two men shouldering rifles step forth into the light.

Behind them stood Erin Moss.

———

"Get out," Jacob said as he quit the car, treading the hard ground as he made his way to the front of the car. The pistol at his side. "Keep close."

Quinn unclipped his seatbelt, stepped out of the vehicle, and came beside him.

"Go on..." he said, gesturing with a hand for Quinn to walk in front.

Quinn walked towards the edge of the road where it met the forest beyond, his hands raised and fingers splayed at the front of his body.

The few steps felt like yards and Jacob checked his corners as he went, expecting little red dots to appear all over his body from hidden guns in the trees, but there were none at all. He kept his eyes and weapon trained on Erin Moss, who welcomed him with a trace of a smile as he stopped right before the small structure that she had emerged from, as though there were some invisible line drawn in the dirt at his feet. Neither of them said anything for a moment. He stood with the gun in his hand.

"Hello, Jacob," said Moss, her arms outstretched to her side as though greeting an erstwhile friend. "Can we put the guns down, please?"

He looked at her, then to the riflemen stood either side of her as he came behind Quinn, using him as a shield. "Sure. You first."

Moss nodded, then the riflemen lowered their weapons. "Nobody's getting hurt today."

"Who are you?" he said, feeling the weight of the gun in his hand as he lowered it.

"You know who I am," she said, as though the question was ill-considered. "But what I *do* is more... complicated."

"Tell me what I'm doing here, Erin?"

Moss glanced over her shoulder at the door behind her. "This is where it all begins for you."

"I don't know this place."

"That's because you're not supposed to," she said, coming closer now. "It's part of the recalibration process."

He shook his head. None of this making any sense. "The *what*?"

"For the past seven years, you've been part of a

progressive pilot trial," she continued. "We call it The Good Citizen program."

"What kind of program?"

"You're not who you think you are, Jacob."

"So people keep telling me."

"Your name is not Jacob Keller," Moss said. "That's the name we gave you."

The stabbing in his head made him wince, and suddenly he felt like he was watching himself from a distance—from the tops of the trees in the forest that surrounded them—watching this whole scene unfold as though it were someone else standing in his place. "Then who am I?"

Moss smiled affectedly. "Your name was Patrick Sullivan before." She reached a hand into her pocket and slowly withdrew a folded sheet of card and held it up for all to see.

He squinted and saw the face printed on the card, which was not a card at all, but a photograph. It was him, only not him *now*. This was the face of another man who looked just like him. A doppelgänger, just less mileage on the face and dressed in a red boilersuit like they wore in jail.

"This was taken seven years ago," said Moss. "Taken after a jury of your peers convicted you for the murder of Alice Taylor and—"

"Who was she?" he said, not letting Moss finish. The name brought forward the face that occupied his most lingering dreams, like an apparition from the next world.

"She's the reason you are here now," Moss said. "She's the reason you volunteered for the program."

His head was a spectral fog, lost between some dream world and reality, but never quite finding either. "You're telling me I killed that woman?" he said, the blur of a memory forming now.

Moss nodded. "Everything you remember, everything after that accident, is not how it seems."

He could feel the hairs on the back of his neck stand on end and hear his heart in his ears. Moss was right. There was something inside him that knew such truths, like some buried ghost trying to crawl its way out of him. "Tell me..."

"Your life now is very different from the one that came before," Moss said, taking care of her choice of words. "You *were* a killer, and your business was death."

He shook his head in disbelief and raised his weapon again, ready to drive a bullet right through her skull. "It ain't true."

Quinn turned to him now and moved his body in front of the barrel. "It is true."

"Why would I kill that woman?"

"Not just that woman. There were others, too."

"Others? Why?"

"Because you were loyal."

"Loyal to who?"

Moss stepped forward again, closing the gap between them with slow and deliberate steps. "The man you used to work for."

It took him a moment to piece it together. "Jimmy Lynch?"

"Yes."

He stood in silence, taking it all in. Running the facts through his head. "Tell me about this program? How does it work?"

"It's hard to explain."

"You took my memories, is that it?"

"It's a little more complicated than that."

"Then make it easy for me."

Moss tilted her head towards the canopy of trees that hung above them, as if pulling strength and succor from the heavens. "We selected you as a candidate when you were in Attica."

"Jail?"

"Yes. As I said, you volunteered."

"Why?"

Moss turned and started back towards the door of the small structure behind her. "For a new life. For a past that you would no longer have to remember." She glanced back over her shoulder, realizing he was still standing there, gun in hand. "Let me show you."

He watched Moss pull open the steel door and disappear back into the blackness beyond. The riflemen followed behind until there was just himself and Quinn left standing in the cold dirt. He waited a second, then gestured for Quinn to lead the way as he followed behind, the pistol welded to his palm as though he and it were one and the same.

The air was heavy and close as he entered, and through the darkened entrance he watched as Quinn descended the flagstone steps to the bottom, then disappear again, down a hallway lit by a faint and flickering sodium lamp. He followed the man down until he came upon a room at the end where he found the four of them stood before a large black monitor mounted on the far concrete wall.

"I know you have lots of questions," Moss said, walking towards the terminal on the desk next to the monitor.

"What is this place?"

"It's nothing now," she said. "But after the Soviet dissolution, this facility became the first research station of its kind."

"For what purpose?"

"The aim of the project was to see if they could decode and encode the human brain."

He repeated the question. "For what purpose?"

"To create a perfect template for humanity. A persona that would abide every moral law written into it."

He gazed upon her shadowed figure, and in that moment, she appeared less a human and more a god. "That can't be possible."

Moss smiled. The kind of smile reserved only for those who had seen a life's work come to fruition. "Many others thought so, too." She let her fingers run across the keyboard. A moment later, a static image appeared on the monitor above them.

It was the faint crackle of audio he heard first. A short lag in the playback as the static image turned to motion.

———

"Can you tell me why you're here?" a voice said.

As the picture sharpened, he could make out two people in the footage. The first figure was himself, sat on one side of a formica table, wearing the same red jail fatigues from the booking photograph Moss had shown him only moments before. The second person—the person speaking—was Erin Moss, sat opposite him. From the position of the camera, which appeared to be mounted to the top corner of one wall, he could only discern the side of her face, poring over the paperwork on the desk in front of her. It was old footage, exactly seven years old, according to the timestamp in the bottom corner of the recording.

"I killed my wife," he said. "But I'm guessing you already know that."

"Can you tell me what happened?"

"I don't want to talk about it."

"Alice?" she said, reading from the report. "Was that her name?"

"Are you deaf? I said I'm not talking about it."

"You have an opportunity here, Patrick. Can I call you Patrick?"

"Call me what you want."

"But I need you to cooperate."

"Why should I? Who are you people, anyway?"

"We're here to help you."

"You can't help me."

Moss paused the footage and looked up at him. "Do you remember that conversation?"

Jacob stood there, unmoving. She knew he didn't. He knew the man in that footage no more than himself right now. A stranger in every mirror. He shook his head and drew in a breath, his stomach turning inside him. Not nausea, but something else. Something deeper. In the shade of the room he stood, his breaths so small he could barely get them out. It was as though he was standing in someone else's shoes, occupying a body that was not his own; a body that no longer belonged to him, but to someone he once knew, long since departed from this world. He was fit to vomit as Moss reached for the terminal again. Another image flashed on the screen, replacing the other, his face the full focus on the monitor now as the gloved hands of some unseen person placed wires on his shaved scalp. His eyes were closed; his face a picture of detached quietude, lost in his own unconsciousness. As the image flicked over to a wider shot, he watched the video play out as his limp body was strapped down to some elaborate machine under bright lights. A dark casket made of strange materials, and from it spewed an array of wires and cables connecting to a cap around his skull. It looked almost unworldly. Masked bodies surrounded the ghost version of himself on the screen. All dressed in surgical scrubs; their faces unseen by the camera beneath the white lights.

"The program was the first of its kind. *You* were the first of its kind," said Moss as she lifted her head to watch the scene play out on the monitor.

"How does it work?" he said, horrified and intrigued all at once.

"The human brain is not just an information processing machine, like many believe. It's an experience machine. It shapes our reality. The way we interpret the world. It's the seat of our consciousness." Moss paused, then pointed a finger back at the monitor. "This is how we mapped your brain."

"And then what?"

"We build an emulation. A copy." Moss looked back at him. "We take out the parts no longer required, and write in the parts that make you who you are now."

He kept his focus fixed on the monitor, trying to work his thoughts into some coherent understanding. Grasping for anything to make sense of it all. "You're telling me that I'm a machine?"

Moss shook her head. "No, I wouldn't look at it that way at all."

"How do you see it, exactly?" He felt his hand tremble; his blood boiling inside him.

"Over the course of our lifetimes, the human body replaces almost every cell it has. Who I am today is not the same person I was last week, or last year. We change all the time. Nothing is immutable. Not our bodies, our minds. Nothing." Moss came around into the light and stood right before him now. "When Theseus sailed home after killing the Minotaur, the Athenians wished to preserve his ship. So, as the old planks rotted, they replaced them with fresh timbers and nails. And as the sails wore out, they raised new ones in their place, until nothing of the old ship remained. Many people agree that, after a time, Theseus' ship was no longer the same ship at all. But no one can quite agree when."

"What is your point?"

"How much has to change before you stop being *you*? Are you still the same person you were yesterday? Are you the same person tomorrow?"

"This is how you justify what you do?"

"Let me ask you a question," said Moss, staring deep into his eyes. "Are you a better person now, or before?"

He looked at Quinn, then back at Moss, unable to answer that question.

Erin Moss let her gaze fall from his. "You're a good man, Jacob. But that wasn't always so."

The dark room in which he found himself seemed to spin. His legs were shaking. "I'm a nobody," he said. "Just a construct that you chose for me."

Moss lifted her head again, which was shaking emphatically from side to side. "You're wrong. You're so much more than that, Jaco—"

"Stop calling me that!" He turned back to face the monitor as the video on the screen continued playing. His unconscious body was prostrate in the machine that they had fastened him to. Entombed like some corpse in a translucent sarcophagus as masked strangers worked around him. Moss reached across the terminal and killed the video. The monitor went black again.

"You don't understand," she said. "You represent everything that society values in a person. The best parts of what human nature has to offer."

"According to who?"

"To all of us."

"But none of it is real. I'm not real!"

"Of course you are. Who you are now doesn't mean you're any less a man than who you were before."

"Who decides what is good and bad? Who decided what I am now?"

The silence that followed was long and filled with awkward glances of ignored truths.

Jacob looked from Moss to Quinn, then back again. "Was it you?"

Moss shook her head and looked to the floor. "It wasn't me."

"Then who?"

Quinn stepped forward and looked up at the object on the screen in which laid the body of Patrick Sullivan. "It's not who," he said. "It's *what*."

Jacob followed his gaze. The translucent casket on the screen was now blinking with various lights and readouts. "What is that thing?"

"It has no official designation," Moss said, looking hard at Quinn, her bottom lip curled in disfavor at his confession. "We call it *Prometheus*."

Jacob swallowed dry. "The god who created man..."

"It's just a name," she said.

"It's not a name, it's a machine."

"Yes, but you are not a machine."

He pressed a hand to the side of his face, the pain in his head like a thousand needle pricks beneath his skull. "What about the dreams?" he said. "They're not dreams at all, are they?"

"We don't know."

"Yes, you do. They're memories, aren't they? From before?"

Moss took in a breath, defeated. "Yes, and no. Unfortunately, the process is gradual. That's why you have the drugs. They're supposed to stop certain information being transferred between neurons until the emulation takes over completely. But some old memories may still slip through."

"So, this machine decides who I am and what I remember. Is that right?"

"If you want to be crude about it."

"My parents? Were they real?"

Moss turned away. "No," she said. "I know what you think of me, but you shouldn't."

"And how is that?"

"Like I said, you were not a good man. But now you are."

He felt his hand shake again as their eyes met and he raised the gun and peered down the gunsight at her darkened face beneath the strip lights. The riflemen raised their weapons in return. "If I shoot you now, that proves whatever you made me was wrong. If I choose to kill you, this whole thing means nothing."

She stared him down, unwavering in her stance. "You're right. But as much as you might want to, you won't do it. Will you?"

He felt his finger reach for the trigger and depress it slightly. Something stopping him from pulling it further.

"Whether you believe it or not, you have a choice," Moss said. "This life, knowing the truth. Or another, where all your wrongdoings are forgotten and you live the life you should have. A free man."

"This is not freedom. This is just swapping one jail for another."

"Freedom is a complicated idea," Moss said. "None of us truly have freedom, as you suggest. All of us surrender some freedom to laws and morals. But you can still be free within those laws."

"It's a lie."

"It's not a lie, Jacob, it's just a different perspective."

He kept the gun raised as he took a step backwards, towards the door he entered and his only way out of this hell. "That's not my name."

He turned and ran and ascended the stairs two at a time until he reached the top and threw open the steel door to the woods. As he stumbled forward, he held up a hand to his eyes and blinked through the mantle of white light that blinded him. When he opened them again, he caught the faint silhouettes of men lined up in a row where the edge of the wood met the road again, each with carbine rifles pressed hard to their shoulders and watching him through their sights. He counted ten at most, then stopped dead in the brushwood. Any hope he had of fleeing this nightmare all but left him in that moment.

"Put the gun down, Jacob." Moss came out from the darkened door with Quinn and the two other riflemen in tow.

He looked up at the sky above him for the longest while, then slowly placed the pistol on the ground. "I want to ask you one more question," he said

Moss nodded. "Go on."

"Down there. You said I was the first?"

"Yes."

"So, there are others like me?"

Chapter 27

Quinn watched from the next room, behind the one-way glass, as Erin Moss syringed the clear liquid into a mainline on Keller's arm.

Keller didn't struggle, and within a few seconds, any sign of wakefulness had all but left him. Quinn looked down at Keller laying there, in the throes of sedated sense-lessness, stretched out on a white table, the man's wrists and ankles manacled to the bedposts, his head fastened by a harness. Keller had surrendered without complaint, but there was a part of Quinn that wished he hadn't come so easily.

"That could have gone a lot worse," said Moss, step-ping into the observation room to join him. She wiped her hands dry on a paper towel. "You did a good."

He said nothing. For the first time, seeing Keller's comatose body tethered to the bed like some animal for slaughter, he felt a sense of unease pass over him. In all the time he had worked on the program, he had only ever seen the before and the after and nothing more. That was how it was supposed to be. The success of the program hinged on its very silence and obscurity, and Jacob Keller was the first example of that. Much like himself, Keller had once loved a woman, and lost her too, albeit by his own hand. For better or worse, Keller could not remember his own deeds and destruction, although the echoes and inevitable marks of his former life appeared to remain hidden between his dreams and nightmares. Keller was the perfect citizen they had hoped for. Erased of all his past sins. And yet, as he stood here, looking down at the face of the killer who he used to be, Quinn realized something. Keller was right: a man stripped of his very nature is no man at all, but a machine. A sleepwalker. Moving through the shadows of a fated existence.

"Mr. Quinn?"

He turned and looked at Erin Moss stood next to him, her head tilted to one side as a look of disquiet fell across her face. He had not heard what she said; his thoughts had drifted elsewhere in that moment.

"Is something the matter?" she said.

There was. It was the reason he had waited for her.

He took out Keller's cellphone and passed it to her. "Read it."

She stared down at the image on the screen as the message opened, then looked up again in horror.

The picture was dark, yet the faces were clear: the boy and the woman, gagged at the mouth and blinded by the camera flash at the moment the photograph had been taken.

Beneath the image was a simple message, time-stamped four hours prior.

"Has anyone else seen this?" Moss said.

"No. I just saw it myself."

Moss started pacing the room.

"What do you want to do about it?"

"There's nothing we can do."

"You can't leave this. These people are not involved."

Moss turned on him. Her face twisted and out of shape. "What do you suggest? We go pick them up? Tell them it was all a misunderstanding? How do we explain that exactly?"

He held her stare but remained calm, collected as ever. "That's not my problem."

"You're right. It's not *your* problem. So let it go."

"The boy is ten-years-old."

She turned on him again, only fire in her eyes. "I said let it go! We have enough to think about without having to worry about his son and latest squeeze."

A long pause followed the reproof, and Quinn looked at Moss as though he had misheard the words uttered in her hot temper. "What did you just say?"

Moss narrowed her eyes and raised her chin slightly. "Excuse me?"

"You said 'his son'..."

"I misspoke."

"No, you didn't."

"I don't have time for this. I'm expecting a call from the Deputy Attorney General any minute."

He grabbed her by the arm and pulled her back from the door. "Why didn't you tell me?" Moss's arm tensed, and he was close enough to feel the warmth of her breath through gritted teeth.

"Because you didn't need to know," she said, her gaze unfaltering. "Now remove your hand."

He released her and stepped back again as she returned the cellphone.

"Look," she said, checking the hallway for prying eyes through the glass hatch in the door. "It wasn't my idea. I voiced my disapproval at the time, but it wasn't my choice to make."

"Why do it? Why put him near the boy?"

"It was a condition of the program. A way to verify its effectiveness on his memory and instinct."

"To see if he recognized him?"

"Something like that. But the boy was barely a year old when it all happened. It was very unlikely either of them would know any different."

Quinn shook his head. "Doesn't make it right."

"I know."

"But you let it happen, anyway?"

"When it was clear that Keller and the boy had started to form a relationship with one another, I asked the committee to consider relocation on ethical grounds. Like I said, it wasn't my decision."

"Then whose was it?"

Moss rubbed her face and drew in a breath. "Listen to me. I have worked for fifteen years to bring this program to fruition, but I still answer to people, just as you do. People who keep the lights on. People who keep you on the payroll. People who won't hesitate to put someone else in charge who will toe the line without question. Someone with fewer scruples."

"That's what you're afraid of? Being replaced?"

"This is my life's work, and I won't stand aside for anybody, or let anyone jeopardize what we've achieved. The price of success is dear, but necessary. You know that more than most."

Quinn stood with his head turned to the floor. "So you'll just let them die?"

Moss cleared her throat and straightened her blouse. "I understand, given your personal situation, that you see things differently. But we cannot run a program of this nature on emotion."

At that moment, Fraser stepped in, straight-backed and wearing a self-satisfied smile. A cellphone in his hand. "He wants to talk to you," he said, passing the phone to Moss.

"This is Moss," she said, taking a breath as she pressed the phone to her ear. "Yes, sir. Thank you."

The room fell silent. Quinn looked on as Moss listened to the voice at the other end of the line, unheard to anyone but her. All blood draining from her face in an instant.

Fraser stood with his hands folded in front of him, his gaze averted, as though he knew exactly the message being delivered to Moss.

Moss shot Fraser a look. Cold and dead. "I would like an opportunity to explain to the committee," she said, speaking into the phone. "No, sir. I understand, but—" Another long silence followed, then Moss lowered the phone without another word and passed it back to Fraser.

"I'll need your access pass," Fraser said, his hand outstretched before the call had ended.

Moss removed the lanyard from around her neck and placed it in Fraser's hand.

"What's going on?" Quinn said, but from the way Moss hung her head, he already knew the answer.

"You'll be taking further instructions directly from me going forward," said Fraser, swapping Moss's access pass with his own.

"Says who?"

"Says the person in charge of correcting this mess."

Quinn looked at Moss. "*He's* in charge now?"

"Yes, I am," said Fraser. "Dr. Moss is relieved of her current duties."

He passed over Fraser's smug face as he turned back to Moss. "Is this true?"

Moss nodded.

"Dr. Moss will stay on in an auxiliary role if she so chooses," Fraser remarked.

Moss rubbed her face once again, then started for the door. "I think we're done here."

"I'm sorry it had to be this way, Erin," said Fraser, watching her go.

"I'm sure you are," she said, leaving the room at a pace.

Quinn followed her down the hallway to the elevators. "Are you heading back to the city?" he asked.

"Not tonight," she said.

"Where are you staying?"

She pressed the call button and waited, trying to hold herself together. "It's not your concern, Marcus."

He waited with her until the elevator doors opened, then got inside.

"What are you doing?" she said.

"I'm coming with you."

"Excuse me?"

"Listen," he said, as they rode the elevator down. "I may not agree with anything that you said back there. But if it's between you and that blowhard running this show, I know who I'd want in the chair."

Her face softened as she looked up at him. "There's a motel close to here. I can get a room for tonight."

"And then what?"

"I don't know. I haven't got that far."

"I'll drive you."

———

The sun was down behind the hills when they reached the motel outside the nearest town. The road was slick and dirty from the filthy rain that had followed them. Quinn pulled into the gravel parking lot and left the engine running. An old sign hung askew in the dusky violet light above the main entrance.

Moss sat with her face to the window, her cheeks sallow as the cabin light flicked on; her sunken eyes in desperate want of sleep. "I'm tired, Marcus."

"I'm sure they've got a room ready for you," he said, looking about the mostly empty parking lot.

"Not that kind of tired."

He turned to look at her, but she kept her gaze fixed towards the hills in the distance, like a woman mourning the days lost to wasted pursuits. "What do you mean?"

"You ever wonder if you made the right choice?"

He took out a cigarette, then offered her the same. "Not a day goes by that I don't."

Moss declined the cigarette with a gentle nod. "And?"

"And what?"

"Did you make the right choice?"

"I'm not sure I ever figured that one out." He rolled the window down and took a pull on the cigarette.

"I often think about all the other lives I could have had instead of this one."

"You and me both." A silent moment of understanding fell over them, then Moss reached across and took the cigarette from his mouth and took a drag of her own.

"My father used to tell me that the price of living is all

the other possibilities you forgo. I never really understood what he meant by that until now."

"None of us understand our parents until we're old enough to see the world as they did," he replied.

Moss held the smoke in her mouth, then closed her eyes as she gently exhaled. "If that's true, then I sure hope I don't live that long."

He smiled as he watched her smoking. Her eyes shut to the world. "Was he good a father?"

"He cared more about appearing to be a good father than actually being one," said Moss, opening her eyes again. "He lived a good-for-nothing life and died in regret. But I don't blame him for that. His life was the lesson I needed in knowing what *not* to do."

Quinn let out a sigh as they sat and listened to the soundless night as the rain finally quieted. "I guess we all make our own mistakes along the way."

Moss turned to look at him as though surprised by the admission. "You have regrets?"

He laughed to himself. "Plenty. It's another conse-quence of getting old."

She discarded the cigarette out the open window, then leaned towards him. "I guess another won't hurt, then."

She kissed him, and he let her, but there was nothing there for him but the smell of smoke on her breath. As she pulled away again, he studied the hangdog expression on her face. Her lips pulled tight together and her eyes dropped in shame. "I'm married," he said.

"I thought you were separated?"

"Still love my wife. Just ain't meant to be anymore."

"But you have needs like the rest of us, right?"

"I ain't even sure what they are anymore."

Moss sighed, then leaned back in her seat. "And people say women are the complicated ones."

He smiled in return and let the moment pass as Moss gathered up her things. "What about you?"

"What about me?" she said, opening the door to leave.

"Regrets?"

Moss shook her head, then quit the car. "Yesterday is gone. And tomorrow, well... tomorrow is uncertain. There's no place for regrets between them."

He watched her go as she crossed the parking lot towards the motel. She never looked back to see him leave.

Chapter 28

He sits with his hands on the wheel of his truck and watches the house from across the street. The lights are on upstairs, and he sees the faint silhouettes of two bodies moving together behind the drawn curtains, caressing one another.

He's got the liquor in him. An empty bottle of whiskey askew on the passenger seat. The gun feels heavier in his hand than normal. He admires the oily glint of black under the streetlight.

When he looks back up at the house again, the light upstairs has dimmed and he can no longer see the shapes of their bodies.

He's out of the truck and walking now, towards the house, and in him broods a sense of mindless violence. His head hurts from the whiskey, and yet it numbs the pain of what he's about to do. He's got the devil in him. Not even God can get in his way.

The next thing he knows, he's standing in the dark of

the bedroom at the foot of a bed, watching her ride another man as if there's no tomorrow.

She's on top of him, her back arched and her head slung back, working him at a steady lick. Her body grinding and writhing to the sound of his heavy groans.

They stop as they both hear the click of the hammer.

The man she's fucking throws her to one side and her first reaction is to reach for the bedsheets until she realizes who it is standing there watching them. What she's hiding beneath the covers is nothing which he hasn't seen before. She is his wife, after all.

"Patrick?" she says, her eyes wide and her face perspiring. Shocked to see the image of her husband in a place he has no place being.

He says nothing back, but holds the stare of the man beside her. He knows this man.

"What the hell are you doing in my house?" the man says, a black look in his eyes, trying to hide his fear at this very moment.

"How long?" he says. Neither of them say a word. He steps closer and raises the gun so it's level with the man's chest.

"Don't do this, Patrick," his wife says, her eyes pleading with his.

"How long?"

"Six months," she says.

He steps closer but cannot feel his body from the whiskey. "You're lying."

"Okay. Ten months. I swear."

His wife is crying now. It's the first time he's seen an ugliness in her that had escaped him before. Everything's a blur. He can't see straight, except for the face of the man he had come to kill tonight.

The man watches him, nostrils flared. "What's it gonna be, Pat?" he says, his back against the headboard as he sits up. "You gonna shoot me?"

"I'm thinking about it."

"You know what it means if you do."

"I know what it means if I don't."

The man says nothing.

"You used to be a brother to me," he says, every limb numb at this point. Tears in his eyes. Then he hears the sound of gentle whimpers spill out from the next room. The tender cries that only a babe could muster. Cries that he had grown to know so well. "Where is my son?"

"He's next door," his wife says, the sheets falling from her breasts as she stands to go to him.

"Sit down!" he says.

"He needs me." She looks up at him with nothing on, only the white garters about her knees. She wipes the tears from her face. "Please?"

"Sit down," he says, letting the barrel of the gun fall about her chest.

She comes at him, baring her teeth. "Are you going to shoot me in front of your son, Patrick?"

"How do I know he's even mine?"

His wife looks at her lover beside her, then back at him standing there. "He is yours. You know that."

"Only thing I know is that his mother's a whore."

Embers flicker in her eyes. Before he realizes it, she's upon him, clawing at his face like a wild animal slipped from its leash. Her teeth find the side of his neck and it sends him staggering backwards.

He sees the man move through the blur of his wife's fists, dick swinging between his legs as he reaches for something atop the side table. A Ruger P90 with a silver slide.

He turns his body and shoves his wife from the line of fire.

She stumbles backwards and falls headlong, the front of her skull hitting the corner of the dresser as she lands.

He fires two shots into the darkness as the man rounds on him. The man stands, limbs frozen as blood finds his eyes, then staggers to the side and leans against the wall, gasping for air. Gutshot and dying. Eyes bulging beneath their sockets as all life leaves him. The bedsheets soaked with gore.

He turns back to his wife, who's lying in a heap on the floor. A swell of red on the carpet beneath her sodden hair. He drops to his knees and turns to her, but there's nothing behind the eyes but small black circles. She doesn't move, not even when he calls her name. She just stares, unblinking.

All that remains is the horrid cry of an infant in the next room.

———

Jacob's eyes flicked open. The image of his wife's lifeless face was the last thing he could remember, carved into his mind like an invisible scar. He had dreamed of her before, many times, but never as clearly as the nightmare from which he'd just awoken.

The strip lights above his head were white hot and blinding and he woke squinting, trying to gather his point of reference. His body was weak as he tried to move, his mind a haze of nothingness. The remnants of whatever drugs they had given him still making their way through his bloodstream.

He tried to lift a hand but couldn't. Then a leg. No luck. Every limb held fast by lengths of black cord to keep him in place.

To the left of him was a tray atop a small table. A scalpel and other medical instruments he could not even name, all lined up in a row.

To the right of him stood the man that had brought him here—the one called Quinn—looking down at him like a specimen laid out on a petri dish, holding an empty syringe in one hand.

"It's a reversal agent," said Quinn, cutting loose the cords that held his body to the bed. "Get up. We don't have much time."

Quinn helped him to his feet as they touched the cold linoleum. He reached out a hand to steady himself on the bed, waiting for the sensation to return to his legs again. "Where are we going?"

Quinn squatted and threw one arm over his shoulder,

taking his weight as he reached for the door. "Getting you out of here."

They stepped out into an empty corridor, the way ahead lit by dim sensor lights as they staggered down a maze of hallways as though tracing some illuminated path to freedom that emerged from the darkness.

At the end of the first hallway, they rounded a corner, leading to a second hallway lined with rows of white cell doors, the viewing hatches left open as faces appeared from the other side, all silent as they watched them pass by like a mourning party.

"This way," Quinn said, as he carried him to the end of the second hallway, then unhanded him to one side as they approached the warden's station at the far end.

The duty warden was sitting with his back to the door beyond the plexiglass, his head buried in a book. Above him, a bank of monitors sat flicking between the cycle of security cameras dispersed about the block. A slow night at the office.

He kept his back to the wall and his face hidden from view as Quinn tapped the window to get the warden's attention.

"Goodnight, Stu." said Quinn.

The warden looked up from his book in mock surprise. "Thought you'd already left for the night?"

"So did I." Quinn held up his keys as though he'd come back for them. "Senior moment."

The warden rolled his eyes and smiled. "Happens to the best of us."

"Say hello to that pretty wife of yours."

The warden raised a brow. "I don't speak to her unless I have to. You know that."

Quinn smiled and followed with a parting nod as the warden reached for the control panel to release the lock on the door to let them out, none the wiser.

When the warden returned to his book, he made quick his exit, his body bent double at the waist so he could keep below the plexiglass window.

They filtered out into a smaller service corridor and kept one eye on the cameras above them as they went, their backs flush to the wall as they worked the dead spots where the cameras couldn't reach.

Quinn swiped his key card across the panel at the end of the service corridor, releasing a second door into a vast atrium at the center of the facility, then paused as he stepped through.

"What is it?" he said.

Quinn held a finger to his lips as the mutter of voices echoed across the high ceilings, growing louder with each footfall, then squatted and pulled him to cover behind a small recess in the wall.

The footfalls drew nearer, then two wardens dressed in uniform crossed by, talking shit and lamenting the cold weather to one another, unaware of the two men hiding in their midst. They watched them pass through another door at the end of the atrium and disappear from view.

As soon as the wardens had gone, Quinn stood again and helped him to his feet. "Let's go."

He followed the man through another set of double doors. Quinn swiped his keycard across the access panel and they pushed through onto the main stairwell. They descended, a step at a time, Quinn bearing the weight of his body as he eased him down, his knees still trying to find their strength. As they hit the landing, another string of voices stirred above them, reverberating off the cold stucco walls.

"We need to move quicker," Quinn said, hauling him down the next flight of stairs.

Jacob placed one hand on the guardrail and threw the other over Quinn's shoulder and struggled down the stairwell as fast as his legs could carry him.

The voices above called out in their retreat, like growling gods from the heavens. They climbed down, towards the last door at the bottom, and hurried through the underground parking lot, towards the black Crown Vic parked crossways in a bay.

Quinn fumbled for the keys as they approached. "Get in."

There was no time to stop. No time to breathe.

"What's going on here?" The voice came out of nowhere.

Jacob shot a look over Quinn's shoulder, his gaze settling upon the wiry figure behind him. He could not make out the face through the shadow, only the wild eyes that glowed through the end of a burning cigarette.

Quinn went still, jaw slack at the sight of the man as he stepped into the light. "Fraser?"

The wiry man looked at him, then at Quinn, and then back again. "Where are you taking him?"

Quinn reached around for his pistol tucked into the waistband of his jeans, then let it hang there for a moment. "Move aside," he said.

The wiry man pulled back, grimacing, noticing the gun. "Think very carefully about what you do next."

As time seemed to stop, all he could hear was the echo of voices again, growing in their chase.

"If you follow us, I'll kill you," said Quinn, his jaw clenched, and all but narrowed slits for eyes.

The wiry man stood expressionless, then retreated again into the shadow with his cigarette.

Quinn took the wheel as they made their exit, hard on the gas as they hightailed it out of there, tires screeching on the resin floor as they went.

Jacob reached for the grab handle to steady himself as they gunned through the main security gate, splintering the barrier in two as they careered into the dark night beyond. "Why are you helping me?" he said.

Quinn shot him a look. A look that promised nothing but bad news. "They have them," he said.

"Have who?"

"The boy. Woman too."

He felt his heart hit his throat. "Lynch?"

Quinn nodded, but his eyes never left the road as the Crown Vic tore through the cold blackness.

"Pull the car over," he said, feeling a knot in his stomach as the nausea came rushing.

"We can't stop here."

"Pull the damn car over!" He quit the car before it had stopped and staggered forwards and vomited his guts up by the edge of the road.

"We can't stay here," Quinn said, still behind the wheel, engine running.

Jacob wiped his mouth dry when he was done blowing chunks into the underbrush, then returned to the car. "How do I find them?"

Quinn reached for the cellphone in his pocket and slid it across, his face cast in blue from the light on the screen as he showed him the photograph. "Wait for their call. Find out what they want."

He studied the image on screen: Amanda and the boy, their mouths gagged and blinded by the camera flash. A bookcase in the back. His apartment. "They want me."

"Then you have to decide whether their lives are worth yours. If you're the kind of man I think you are now, then I already know the answer."

They sat in silence. Nothing but the sound of the wind through the trees and the start of yet more rain.

"There's something else you need to know," said Quinn, eyeing the road ahead again as he stepped on the gas.

"Go on..."

Quinn turned to him now, a grim look in his eye. "It's about the boy."

———

They drove on, hard and fast, and picked up the flooded highway north, listening to the rain on the windshield as it fell in sheets. Jacob checked the cellphone. There had been no further messages from Lynch. No time. No location. Nothing.

"They'll call you," Quinn said, as certain as a man could be. "Give it time."

He sat back in the seat and looked out to a night as black and angry as his turn of mind. The man next to him had just told him that the boy was his son. He had no reason to trust him, and despite the naked truth of it all, he had a hard time believing it. His mind was wandering in places it had never been before. Thoughts that he had never thought possible. He was a father, and that alone was enough to make his blood run cold. Not because he was afraid of what he meant to the boy, but because of what the boy meant to him. "Maybe they're already dead..." he said.

Quinn glanced over at him, then back at the road again. "They ain't dead."

"Why are you helping me?"

Quinn cleared his throat. "Because I know what it's like to lose a child," he said, his voice broken and toneless beneath the stains of grief that plagued his countenance. "And since you're going to ask next, it was a hit and run. Never found who did it."

"I'm sorry."

"So am I."

Another mile passed before he asked the question. "How old was she?"

"A week before her sixteenth. Happy fuckin' birthday, sweetheart."

Quinn slowed the car as the blinking lights of a motel sign lit up a small strip of sky ahead, just visible through the squall. They pulled into the parking lot with the headlights dimmed.

Jacob took it all in. A few station wagons and an old RV parked up across the way. "What are we doing here?"

"She's in that room up there," said Quinn, pointing to a room on the upper floor of the motel, a soft amber light escaping the fringes of the drawn curtains.

"Who?"

"You know who."

He sat watching the window of the motel room for a while. "Erin Moss?"

Quinn nodded.

"Does she know we're coming?"

Quinn shook his head this time.

Jacob felt a sudden coldness come over him, as though all the blood had been drained from his body. His thoughts strayed into an empty void as he looked up at the motel room again and gave thought to what he would do next. He felt a coldness run down his arms to the tips of his fingers, and when he lowered his head again, he saw Quinn's hand move slowly away to reveal the pistol he had placed on his lap.

Quinn rolled down the window and smelled the rain

riding the air. "You asked why I'm helping you," he said. "I never got the chance to save my daughter, or kill the sonofabitch that took her from me."

He let the thought of the boy linger for a moment as he held the gun and turned it in his hand. He looked out across the parking lot at the motel room once more and stepped out of the car into the rain.

"I'll be here," Quinn said, leaning across to speak. "Whatever you decide."

He studied the pistol again as the rain lashed against his back, then walked for the stairwell towards the rooms on the upper level.

Chapter 29

She hadn't noticed him sat in the chair in the corner of the room when she came out of the bathroom, a towel wrapped around her body as her damp hair sat limp around her shoulders.

He sat in the quiet darkness as she reached for the light switch on the wall, her back to him, then cocked the hammer on the pistol to make his presence known. Her whole body went stiff at the sound of it. The sudden realization that there was another person in the room with her. "Turn around," he said.

Erin Moss turned slowly to face him, following the trail of wet boot prints on the faded carpet to the corner of the room where he was sitting.

He looked up at her from the chair, rainwater running off his chin like a sluiceway.

Moss tried to speak, but no words came out, as though someone had cut out her tongue as she got the measure of him.

"Why are you scared of me?" he said.

Moss finally found her voice. "Should I be?"

"You tell me." His jaw cut a jagged shape against the dark brown walls. "You programmed me to think and do what you want. So, why are you scared?"

He could see the lump in her throat as she swallowed. The sudden reality of this moment passing over her. Her skin was wet across her shoulders from the shower. "A man can do what he desires," she said. "It's only *what* he desires that he has no choice about."

He studied her closely, unmoving. "Sit down."

Her eyes went first to the door, then to the window at the back of the motel room, assessing her options. "I'll stand."

"Suit yourself." He stood now, pistol in hand, and went to the window by the door. Outside, the rain was coming down like black tendrils. The parking lot glistened like an oil slick beneath the streetlamps.

Moss steadied herself, keeping her back flush to the wall as she kept her distance. "How did you get out?"

"Doesn't matter."

Her eyes narrowed as she gave thought to it, edging closer to the door as he walked back into the room again. "Quinn?"

He watched as one of her hands fell to her side, the doorknob at her fingertips now. "Door's locked," he said, holding up the room key.

Moss's face went whiter than the towel that sheathed her state of undress. She was vulnerable and looked every part the harried quarry at the mercy of her huntsman.

He walked back to the window and pulled the curtains to check outside again. Nothing but driving rain and Quinn's car still parked with the lights on. "I had a thought..." he said, turning to face her again, his body soaked to the bone.

Her voice was impossibly small. Almost a whisper. "Go on."

"If I kill you now, that proves your program was a failure."

"Maybe."

"Maybe?"

"Yes. Are you going to kill me?"

"I'm not responsible for my actions. I am the way I am because of you. Right?"

She held his gaze for a moment and repeated the question. "Are you going to kill me?"

"I'm thinking about it."

"Don't think too long," she said, her expression hardening suddenly. "Either get on with it, or get out."

"I want you to tell me something."

She came forward, chin raised. "What?"

He reached a hand into his pocket and withdrew the photograph that had come to define his forgotten past. "Who is *she*?" he said, his finger falling on the image of the woman he knew only as Alice Taylor.

Moss studied the photograph in his outstretched hand. "You know who she is."

"I want to hear it again."

"She was your wife."

"Right," he said, returning the picture to his pocket. "But who else was she?"

She held his stare but drew a blank. "I don't follow."

"She was the mother of my child, wasn't she?"

Moss averted her gaze. "Yes."

He studied the photograph again, then wiped the rain from his face. "I didn't mean to kill her."

She looked up at him again, her eyes dancing with interest. "Then you remember?"

"Maybe. But I want you to tell me."

"Tell you what?"

He came closer and perched himself at the foot of the bed, the chenille bedspread neatly made. "The truth."

She took in a breath and steeled herself. "Your wife was leaving you for another man. That's it."

"What man?"

"Eddie Lynch. The brother of the man you worked for. I don't think I need to explain the rest."

He shook his head, unsure if he heard that correctly. "His brother?"

Moss pulled the towel up around her body to keep it from falling. "Now you know why Jimmy Lynch wants you dead."

He felt his heart quicken, head already throbbing. "He has my son."

"I know," she said. "What do you want me to do here, Jacob? I can't help you now."

"Tell me what happened to him?"

"Your son?"

"Yes. What happened to him after..." He couldn't bring himself to utter such crimes and lurkings of inner evils.

"After you killed his mother?"

"Yes."

Moss looked down at the shape of the gun in his hand as he stood there. "The woman who raised him *is* the boy's aunt, if that's what you mean."

"She had a sister?"

Moss held the towel tight around her body with one hand and swept her damp hair away from her face with the other. "It took us a while to find her. Your wife hadn't seen or spoken to her in years. Since their mother died, in fact. It was enough to tear them apart."

"But she took him in?"

"It took some convincing."

"How much?"

"Fifty thousand."

"You paid her?"

"She wanted nothing to do with him at first, but you wanted the boy to stay with family. You knew your wife had a sister somewhere, so we found her. We made the arrangements you asked for."

"What did you tell her?"

"We told her that your wife died in a house fire. She never questioned it."

He looked out of the window again. "Did you know she was an addict?"

"She was sober at the time."

"And you're sure he's my son?"

Moss never missed a beat. "We tested," she said. "He's yours."

He stepped away from the window for the last time, unlocked the door, then placed the room key atop the side table. He looked up at Moss, noticed the slight drop in her shoulders and the small breath of relief as it left her. "If you come looking for me," he said, "I will finish what I came here to do."

And with that, he was gone, into the night; into the rain that swallowed him, his boots pounding hard in the pools of rainwater as he walked back out into the parking lot where Quinn was waiting for him.

———

Quinn sat with the phone to his ear, listening to the usual voicemail play out against the heavy fall of rain on the windshield.

"*Hey, this is Chloe. I can't find my phone right now, so I'll call you back. Unless it's my dad, in which case, I'm still looking for it. Leave a message if you want.*"

At the beep, he started talking. "Hi, sweetheart. I got nothing to say, really. Just wanted to hear your voice..." From the corner of his eye, he saw a shape moving through the squall, the face obscured under the shadow of a hood as Keller walked heavily towards him, like some wearied soldier pelted by a hail of shrapnel. "Sorry, I gotta go. I miss you."

He returned the cellphone to the console tray and watched as Keller opened the passenger door and got in. Keller was silent for a long while as he caught his breath and wiped the rain from his face.

He let the man gather himself and tried to read the room. "We good?"

Keller never looked at him as he placed the pistol in the glove compartment. "Yeah. We're good."

He hadn't heard gunshots. Just rain. And as he looked up, he saw a face at the window of the motel room looking out, half-hidden behind the drapes. Erin Moss watched them for a moment, then disappeared back inside again. "Tell me where we're going?" he said, firing up the Crown Vic and letting it idle for a moment.

Keller turned to face him now. The whites of his eyes had turned red, and his expression was as black and bitter as the night he was chasing. There was only one reasoned answer. Only one a father would say. "To get my son back."

Chapter 30

The message from Lynch came through within the hour.

Jacob opened the link on his cellphone and a pin dropped onto the map on the screen. The location of the meet would be at an old disused warehouse south of the city, right below the Walt Whitman Bridge, to the east of the navy yard overlooking the grim waters of the Delaware River.

He rode shotgun as Quinn drove, and the rain fell without end as the headlights swept across the highway as though they were cruising upon a vast oil spill. They picked up the Schuylkill Expressway from the exit near West Conshohocken and drove the twenty miles south until they reached the city. Neither man spoke. There was nothing left to be said.

"Take the next exit," he said.

Quinn steered the car towards the off ramp at Exit 350, eyes narrowed as he leaned into the wheel to see through the deluge, the wipers nothing but a blur as they see-sawed across the windshield to clear the way.

"Left at the lights," he continued, checking the nav system on the cellphone as they approached the intersection at Packer Avenue and South Darien Street.

On green, Quinn pulled a left and drove east down Packer, then reached a hand down beside him and presented a small switchblade that he'd kept hidden in the map pocket of the door. "Take this."

Jacob took it and turned it as he studied the blade. "Ain't much use against buckshot."

Quinn smiled. "You need to get that thing out of your arm."

He looked down at the blade again and turned his arm to feel the small lump of the tracker beneath the skin. There wasn't any city or slum in the world where they couldn't find him. All it would take was the stroke of a few keys. He pressed a forefinger to the point of the blade and drew blood, then lowered the edge across the inside of his upper arm, feeling the corners of the tracking device buried under the flesh next to the pit of his arm. The blade sliced through his skin like butter, and a small trail of blood traced its way down his arm to the crook of his elbow. He twisted the point carefully underneath the tracker, making a small incision, just big enough to work the tracker loose.

Quinn averted his gaze as he withdrew a small rectangular chip from his arm. No bigger than the size of a fingernail.

Jacob studied it between his bloodied fingers for a moment, then rolled down his window and let the wind carry it off somewhere into the blackness. "Do you have any idea what we're walking into?"

Quinn shook his head and pulled at his tie to loosen it, then worked another button free on his shirt. "Do you?"

"I don't know these people. Not anymore." The cold air on his face felt bracing as he rolled the window up again.

"As I see it, we don't have much of a choice. Not if you want to see them alive again."

Jacob checked the clock on the dash, holding the sleeve of his shirt against the fresh wound to stem the bleeding. "We're already late." He felt his body jerk back into the seat as Quinn stepped on the gas, the needle moving to ninety as the chassis shook in the high wind.

"Whatever happened back there," said Quinn, "you should know that she did what she did for the right reasons."

"That a fact?"

"I know Erin well enough to understand her intentions came from a good place."

"Is this the part where you say she tried to help me?"

Quinn looked at him, then at the road again. "Not just you."

He leaned his head against the window and watched the flecks of rain cluster on the glass. "Good place or not, only God gets to make that choice."

"You believe such things?"

"I don't know."

"Well, if he exists, he didn't much care for either of us."

They followed the road onto South Delaware Avenue, past a stack of shipping containers and cranes lining the bank of the river to the left of them. The entrance to the warehouse was hidden off an unmarked access road, next to a row of cement storage domes and chutes that had turned to rust from the weather. The place was quiet. There was nothing out here except for the remains of an old-world industry that had long been brought to ruin.

"Stop the car," he said, as the shape of the abandoned building appeared through the gloom. There was no light. No other cars, from what little he could see. As Quinn slowed the vehicle to a stop on the rough ground, he reached back into the glove compartment for the pistol. He stepped out into the cold, heart pounding as he felt the heel of his boot sink into the mire beneath him. For a long moment he just listened, an ear to the wind, waiting for a sound that might give a position away. Up close, the derelict warehouse sat like a ruined monument of a bygone era; built on land that had long gone to seed. "Let's go," he said, treading mud as he cut a path to the entrance of the building.

Quinn walked to the rear of the Crown Vic and opened the trunk. He grabbed a flashlight and looked down at the twelve gauge pump-action shotgun he kept in the aluminum trunk case, next to another case housing an

AR15. He took the shotgun and shouldered it, then lit a path ahead as he came behind.

The double doors to the warehouse were ajar as they approached, swinging on the hinges in the crosswind. Jacob raised the pistol as he entered, his back pressed flat to the brick wall as he traced the edge of the building, eyes struggling in the darkness as Quinn swept the floor with the flashlight. "Stay behind me." He edged further into the building, broken glass and debris crunching underfoot. The place was cold and damp and there was a lingering smell of wet rot in the air from the decaying timbers that just about kept this place standing. They moved from room to room, each one darker than the last; each one just as empty. Nothing but rats scurrying for the darkness. There was no sign of life anywhere, just the whistling of the wind through the rafters, and the scuttling of critters in their flight. As he turned again, he saw Quinn with a finger pressed to his lips, stock still where he stood, eyes lifted to the ceiling, tracing the moving shadows from an old light cord that swayed in the wind through the broken windows.

"Did you hear that?" Quinn said, his voice impossibly low. "Upstairs."

He listened for a moment—nothing but the wind at first—and then he heard it. The creak of floorboards above them. A slow rocking sound right above their heads. He made for the door. Quinn followed. They pressed on through the ruined building until they happened upon a large vestibule with a concrete staircase at the far end. He moved towards the staircase as Quinn fanned the flash-light from wall to wall. Still nothing.

He started up the steps, keeping his head turned upward, eyes alert to anything lurking above as his spine traced the contours of the wall so he could see past the bends. He stopped at the halfway mark, realizing the only footfalls he could hear were his own.

Quinn was still standing at the bottom, unmoving. He pointed back to the way they'd come and then to his ear to signal that he'd heard something else in another room below. "You go up," he said. "I'll cover here." And then he was gone.

Jacob pressed on, climbing the rest of the stairwell to the next landing. At the top, the floor opened out onto a long corridor which ran either side of him. Total black-ness at both ends. He glanced right and narrowed his eyes to see the small patch of moonlight on the floor from the window at the far end, and nothing else but a line of open doorways into what he figured were the old offices of this fallen empire. To his left was the same. Door upon door into yet more darkened offices. Directly in front of him was yet another door. The only one pulled shut.

He crept forward, stepping to the side of the door in front of him so that his body was slightly left of it, and checked his shoulder. Quinn was nowhere in sight. He kept the pistol raised, both hands on the grip, then lowered one to reach for the doorknob.

A skin-slapping explosion flooded the room, followed

by a second. The loud report of a ten-gauge shotgun cut through the silence like a waking giant.

He recoiled at the noise, eardrums ringing as the door in front of him splintered on its hinges. He unhanded the pistol, which went sliding across the broken floorboards.

A moment later, an enormous figure stepped out from the other side of the door, bearing the shotgun between his arms and moving like a brute through the darkness. As the figure turned, he saw nothing but the whites of his eyes flash through the gun smoke, racking another shell.

Jacob lurched forward as the barrel of the shotgun took aim at his chest, and he grasped for the muzzle with one hand and let fly with the other.

His attacker staggered two steps to his rear as he landed both blows to the side of his unseen face, then he twisted loose the shotgun and landed a further parry of hooks, feeling the crack of his attacker's mandible some-where amongst it all as his fist connected with his jaw. Then the sound of teeth being spat to the floor.

He felt a shooting pain through his thigh as all his weight shifted onto his wounded leg and his grip on the shotgun muzzle gave way, giving enough space for his attacker to regain his own footing.

And then the man was upon him again, the full force of the brute behind the blow to his body. He heard the crack of a rib but the pain didn't follow, and as he looked up again, beyond his attacker's shoulder, he spotted another figure step forward into the faint light through the dusty window at the opposite end of the corridor, moving towards them with a hollering no less than a war cry.

He reached with both hands and pulled his attacker towards him, so close he could smell the tobacco on his breath.

The report of three more gunshots split the air: .45 ACP's by the sound of it.

He fell backwards, bearing the full weight of his attacker as they hit the deck. The shockwave of the three rounds repeating as they punched a hole right through his attacker's chest.

The back of his skull hit the floor as he went down, followed by two hundred pounds of dead weight right on his chest that punched all the air out of him.

He rolled his attacker's lifeless corpse to one side, then turned to see the HKP30L on the floor next to him. A fingertip distance as he stretched an arm out.

A fourth round went up as the second gunman loomed out of the darkness, the shot ricocheting next to his leg.

With a final heave, he pushed the bulk of the dead man off his chest and grasped for the fallen pistol beside him, then twisted his body slightly so he could take aim, weapon trained on the large black mass moving towards him at a pace.

He pulled the trigger, both rounds punching holes in the drywall as the shooter took cover behind a doorjamb.

He scrambled to his feet again, gun raised as he pitched forwards, feeling the trickle of something wet down the back of his neck, his hand damp with what felt like blood as he pressed a palm to the back of his skull.

The shooter appeared again, moving like a shadow from the cover of the door, followed by two more shots.

He blinked through the muzzle flash as he let off another round of his own. No sound of drywall this time, just a small whimper from the darkness, but not enough to put the man down.

He fell to one knee as he went to walk. A sharp pain in his thigh where one of the shooter's rounds had clipped him in return.

He glanced up to see the shooter darting from cover again, heading back up the corridor from which he'd arrived. On his feet again, he limped as fast as his wounded leg could carry him, stepping over the corpse of the first shooter. He took aim once more, looking for the center mass of the retreating shadow as he staggered towards the end of the hallway, but lost sight of him as the gunman vanished into the darkness again. He followed after him, down the flight of steps of a smaller stairwell towards the ground level, leaning hard on the balustrade to take the weight off his punctured leg. At the bottom, he came to another large room. Quiet. Empty. As dark as the rest of it. He popped his head round the corner to steal a look. Nothing.

"Jacob?"

The voice made him jolt as he turned to it.

Quinn was standing behind him, hidden beneath the recess in the stairwell.

"You see where he went?" he said.

Quinn pointed at the floor, picking out the trail of blood spatters leading to the door at the far end.

"Wait here," he said. "Don't move." He checked his clip. One round left in the chamber.

There was more blood streaked across the walls. Arterial spray, if he had to guess, which meant that the shooter wouldn't be going anywhere in a hurry. He followed the trail of blood through the door, spotting more dark spatters in the dirt. An SUV was parked a hundred yards ahead, beneath an awning which had collapsed at one end. He circled the outside of the vehicle, the blood now swelled to a pool by the rear wheel.

The shooter was sitting with his back against the fender, struggling to load the fresh magazine into his weapon. His hand was shaking; his breaths were short and shallow. Nothing to them. The side of his neck and shirt collar blackened with blood.

The shooter looked up at him as he came forward and dropped the magazine to the ground beside him. He tried to raise his weapon, but was barely strong enough to lift his own hand from his lap.

There was a *click* as the shooter dry fired into the darkness.

He came closer as the man spat blood from his mouth, all hope gone from his expression. The look of a man who knew his fate. "Where are they?"

The shooter spat a second time, choking on his own mucus.

He asked again. "Where are they?"

The shooter's gun fell from his hand, the look of a dying man. Eyes glazed over. The last gasps of breath.

He squatted and watched the life fade from him until there was nothing left but the corpse which remained in his place.

———

Quinn was gone when he returned. The recess underneath the stairwell now abandoned where he had left him. Then he heard his voice from upstairs.

"Get up here."

He limped back up the stairwell, checking for anyone else who might be lurking and had yet to make their presence known.

Quinn was standing in the doorway in the center of the corridor where the first gunman had come blasting through with his shotgun and almost taken his head off not a minute before, the splintered remains of the door at his feet. There was nothing but pure dread on his face.

Jacob limped over like a lame mare and wiped the sweat from his forehead on the back of his shirtsleeve. Quinn didn't bother to look up at him as he approached, his gaze transfixed on something else in the room before him.

In the center of the empty office was the slumped shape of a woman hanging by her arms from the rafters, head bowed as if in mourning; her naked body swinging in the faint light.

Jacob eyed the silver necklace around her neck, the tips of her toes almost stroking the floor. She did not move.

Quinn reached for his arm to hold him back as he stepped in. "Don't go in there."

"I have to." There was a sudden coldness to the room that he hadn't noticed before. A draft coming in from a broken window. The smell of gun smoke. A handful of discharged shells and casings scattered about the floor. He thought she was dead before he laid a hand on her, but Amanda's skin was still warm to the touch as he raised a finger to the side of her neck, feeling for a pulse. There it was, shallow and thready, but the rhythm was still there. He came round so that he was now standing and looking up at the front of her; her face hidden behind a veil of bloodied hair; her chin pressed to her chest and her head lolled to one side as though it could fall right off her naked body. He unbound her wrists from the chains and removed her necklace as he took the weight of her tiny frame and eased her down onto the filthy floor. As he pulled back her hair, he turned his gaze to the side, unable to look at her swollen face.

"She's alive," said Quinn, removing his jacket as he came in and placed it on top of Amanda's body. "We need to get her to a hospital."

Jacob took her head in his hands and gently stroked the side of her cheek. Her eyes struggled open and searched the darkness for his face. "I'm here," he said, and she heard him.

Amanda opened her mouth to speak, but she was too weak to say anything. She shut her eyes again, drifting in and out of consciousness.

"Don't say anything," he said, holding her in whatever warmth his arms could muster.

When he got to his feet again, the cellphone rested on the small table at the back of the room started to ring.

"You want me to answer?" Quinn said, taking up the phone.

Jacob eased Amanda's body to the floor again, then stood with his hand outstretched. "It's for me." He lifted the phone to his ear but said nothing. He could hear the caller's labored breaths over the broken line, and he recognized the voice when it finally spoke.

"I take it you got my message?" said Lynch.

"She had nothing to do with this," he said, his hand shaking with rage.

"Maybe. But we're both men of reputation. Would you agree?"

"I don't agree with anything you've gotta say."

"You always were weak around women, Patrick. Guess that's why they end up like they do."

"Where's the boy?"

"He's safe. For now. Good kid." Lynch inhaled sharply, as if smoking a cigarette. "And my men?"

"What do you think?"

"That's too bad. I was just starting to like this kid."

"You touch him and I'll make sure the rest of your brief life will be nothing short of a living hell."

"I don't doubt it," Lynch said, unwavering in his response. "But I was just telling him all about you, in fact."

"You would have killed him already if you were going to."

Lynch laughed. "I never like to show my hand too early."

"Let him go."

"You're not in a position to be making demands here."

"Tell me what you want?"

There was a long pause and more labored breaths.

"What you owe me," Lynch said. "Your life."

There was another silence now as Quinn came beside him, listening.

"Your life for the boy's life," Lynch said. "Fair trade."

"How can I trust you to keep your word?"

"You can't. But you'll come, anyway."

He squatted beside Amanda's beaten body and held her hand in his. "Where?"

"Wait for my message. I'll send a meet point," Lynch said. "And Patrick? For the kid's sake, be on time."

He stayed kneeling and listened to the dead tone on the other end of the line for a moment as Quinn stood over him, then wrapped a hand underneath Amanda's body and stood with her in his arms. "Let's go."

Chapter 31

He cradled her body in his arms on the back seat and brought a hand to her cheek and stroked it with a gentle brush of his finger. "I'm right here," he said, his voice a whisper, watching her eyes slowly blink open to meet his.

Amanda drew in a broken breath, tears in her eyes; her mouth too swollen to speak.

He parted her bloodied fringe from her face and managed a smile. "Don't speak."

She swallowed and reached a hand out for his as the passing streetlights laid bare her waning shape and the fading light in her eyes.

He felt her frail grip on his arm as she closed her eyes again, as though surrendering to whatever force that was trying to steal her from this world. He raised her head slightly to keep her awake as her grip slackened on his arm. "Just a little longer," he said, pulling her close to his chest as he looked up at Quinn at the wheel and glimpsed the man in the rearview. "Hurry..."

Quinn pulled the Crown Vic onto the next street, hard on the wheel, his foot to the floor as the tires fought for purchase on the blacktop. They hightailed it down the straight, back past the sea containers stacked aloft in the yard. The filthy black of the river just beyond. Quinn opened up the throttle as they careered beneath the underpass of the Walt Whitman Bridge, the car rocking and pitching from the cracks in the road, engine rattling as they gunned the red light and pulled a hard left onto Packer Avenue, over the decaying railroad tracks, and into another left onto Christopher Columbus Boulevard. They took the road south, the road north towards Whitman blocked by a jackknifed semi-truck that had spilled its contents onto the road.

The rail yard to the right of them was nothing but a blur as they tore through the crossing at Pattison, the lights flashing red in the darkness beneath the crossbuck as the wishbone gates came down. They drove on, then Quinn was hard on the horn as he pulled the speeding car alongside a slowing pickup truck ahead of them, the side mirror shattering on the rear end of the trailer as the Crown Vic swerved to avoid it. Jacob pitched forward in his seat as the vehicle accelerated into the oncoming lane, passing the line of traffic in front, the tires still slipping on the road, leaving a spray of rainwater in their wake as they headed towards LoMo.

Amanda's head lolled to one side and her body went

limp. He shook her in his arms and held her tighter. "Stay with me," he said, trying to raise whatever life she had left in her.

Quinn, eyes laser-focused on the road, barreled past the thinning traffic as they converged on the quiet, old-school South Philly neighborhood, his foot never leaving the gas as the Crown Vic flew down Broad Street, heading north through Marconi Plaza, past the shuttered shops and row homes that lined that street, never slowing for the intersections as cars broke and spun sideways to miss them.

The sign for Jefferson Methodist Hospital fell into view. Quinn pulled the car to the curb, brake lights dancing across the side of the buildings opposite.

Jacob spilled out on the sidewalk and hoisted Amanda's body into his arms once more and carried her inside. He didn't hear what Quinn said as he hurried towards the entrance. He couldn't think straight. He was acting on pure, frenzied instinct. Everything else seemed to melt away into oblivion.

A sea of solemn faces dressed in scrubs greeted them as he lurched through the doors, the pain in his leg searing and almost giving up on him. Amanda's naked body was bent double in his arms; her skin was a horrid patchwork of black and purple swelling under the white-hot strip lights.

An orderly rushed at him and grabbed an empty gurney left abandoned in the corridor. He eased her down onto the bed, sweat pouring down the back of his neck as he tried to catch a breath, the lights blinding.

The orderly threw a sheet over Amanda as more bodies dressed in white coats and scrubs came out from their rooms to assist.

"Can you tell me what happened?" a doctor asked, calm but firm as she wheeled the gurney down the corridor. Another checked for vital signs.

He paused as all faces turned to him. He was wordless. Unable to form a sentence.

"Was she hit? A car?" the doctor said, her patience already waning.

He found his head shaking. A sudden reflex as a dozen eyes bore into him. "I'm not sure."

"Do you know her?"

He nodded and studied the doctor's stony stare behind the mask. "Her name's Amanda."

The doctor's eyes narrowed as she studied him, his bloodied hands. "But you don't know what happened?"

He stopped as they carried Amanda off into a side room and yet more bodies piled in, drawing curtains, leaving just him and the doctor in the corridor.

The doctor stood watching him for the longest moment, then removed her mask. She was young but wore a face tired beyond her years. "Sir, I need you to tell me what happened." Her calmness was at once replaced with a palpable unease, her hands shifting for the phone atop the nurses' station beside her.

He steadied himself, short of breath and struggling for air. His throat was narrowing with each passing second, as though a noose had been placed around his neck and tightened fast. He stepped backwards, down the corridor that he'd entered from. Towards the exit. Gasping for the bitter air that his lungs were fighting for. "Don't let her die," he said, his eyes never leaving the young doctor's as she watched him go.

The cold air hit his lungs as he staggered back out onto the sidewalk. He inhaled sharply, his body numb to the core and his brain beating inside his skull.

Quinn shot him a look as he limped towards the Crown Vic, his expression as solemn and unsmiling as the dim face of the black sky under which this night had become known. "What happened?"

"Just drive!" he said as he fell into the seat.

Quinn checked his mirrors and started the engine.

Then they were gone, vanishing into the darkened streets towards Center City.

———

Ten minutes later, they found themselves propped up at a dive bar overlooking Passyunk Square. The bar was quiet, save for a couple of old Joe's at the bar with their bowl of potato skins waiting for any young and willing lady to come along and lend an ear to the whispers of their filthy tongues.

Jacob leaned forward across the bar and sipped his

glass of beer as Quinn rolled himself a cigarette. "Those things will kill you," he said.

Quinn looked at him askance. "That's the plan," he said, returning to his roll. "Besides, no one respects a quitter."

He sipped his beer again, then turned his attention back to the big screen on the wall. A Phillie's game playing.

"What's the plan?" Quinn said, placing his hand-rolled cigarette behind his ear. One for the road.

"There's no plan."

Quinn raised a brow in his direction. "You're just going to give this man what he wants?"

He considered it, then nodded. "I guess that's the plan, after all."

A bargirl appeared and collected his empty glass. Big eyes and the breasts to boot. "Another?"

Quinn beat him to the response. "No, we're heading off." The bargirl rolled her eyes and disappeared out the back. "There has to be another way?" he said, standing from his tool.

"What would you do?"

"I don't know. I never was much a thinking man."

"Then you're no help to me."

"I know one thing, though. You ain't gonna find the answer at the bottom of a glass. Seems to me you didn't come this far just to come *this far*."

Quinn was right. He'd already left Amanda. Didn't know if he'd ever see her again. Didn't know if she'd ever want to. If she made it through the night, there would be a chance for her. If he made it, maybe a chance for the both of them. The boy too.

"I'm going for a piss," said Quinn, turning on his heel. "I hope you find those stones you're lacking while I'm gone."

He watched Quinn file out, past the walls lined with Pearl Jam prints and the band setting up on the corner stage. Then the cellphone atop the bar started to ring. An unknown number. He answered it. "I'm listening..."

"4701 Fort Mifflin Road." The voice on the other end was rough. "Keep going until you get to the underpass. Be there in an hour."

He felt his skin chill and his blood run cold, his thoughts racing. "Not until I hear the boy. I want proof of life."

There was a long pause, the silence filled with heavy breaths. "Hold on..."

Another silence. The sound of footfalls. A door opening. Keys in a lock. Then came the small voice he'd been waiting for.

"Hello?"

Hearing the boy made him shake. He closed his eyes, all the blood in his body rushing to his limbs. "Ben? Are you okay?"

A second passed. "I'm okay."

He let out a sigh and gave silent thanks to whatever blessed power cared to listen. "I'm coming to get you," he said, yet his words went unanswered; the boy's voice now lost and gone to the dead tone on the other end. He returned the cellphone to his pocket, his body pumping with adrenaline, toiling in the silent thoughts that followed. He imagined the boy all alone, holed up in some filthy and airless room with no sense of time or place. But the boy was alive, and that was all he needed to know.

"Was that him?"

He lifted his head to see Quinn stood next to him, hands in his pockets as though minutes had passed without notice.

He nodded.

"Are you ready?"

He nodded again.

"And the boy?"

"He's alive."

Quinn placed the cigarette on his lips. "How long do we have?"

"One hour. Fort Mifflin Road. Do you know it?"

"I know it."

"How far is it from Jimmy Lynch's place?"

"Not too far. Why?"

He got to his feet and quit the bar. "Because I need to ask you to do one last thing for me."

Chapter 32

Quinn took the exit off the I95 and drove south on Island Avenue, past the stretch of depots and old terminals that bordered the highway. Above him flickered the lights of airplanes in flight, and the roaring engine of a 747 with three hundred souls on board. He took a right towards Fort Mifflin and followed the dark highway past the vast apron of Philadelphia International that sat like a brilliant jewel to the right of him.

The Crown Vic shook as the wings of a monstrous bird came right above him now, its landing gear down in its descent, falling fast below the cloud that hung about the land like a fallen shroud, towards the runway lights that strobed like silent beacons on the landing strip.

He drove on, following the fence line that bent with the highway and the trees all around him stood like watchmen against the blue-black sky, the first signs of a new dawn appearing through a break in the sky to the east.

Sunup was upon him, but that was the only fact of which he was certain. Perhaps he'd live to feel the sun touch his face again. Perhaps he wouldn't. Either way, he wasn't far now.

The man he had come to call his equal had asked one last thing of him when he'd left him on the sidewalk outside the sprawling Lynch residence: to collect the boy and take him some place far from here. Jacob Keller had made him spit on it. An oath between strangers with nothing else to pledge but his word. So that's what he agreed to do. To get the boy. What happened next was up to Keller.

And what happened to him was up to God.

The underpass appeared out of nowhere as he rounded the last bend in the road. He slowed the car to a stop and scoped the place, lights on, engine running. Behind him was nothing but an empty highway. The same ahead of him.

He sat and watched the empty highway with the windows down, taking in the sound of the night and the cold breeze that carried with it the bite of winter off the river.

A shaft of headlights swept across the highway opposite, finding their way through the darkness as two Lincoln Navigators approached at a crawl.

This was it.

Quinn turned the gun in his hand and looked up as the two Navigators came to a stop beneath the dim lights of the underpass. He pushed the car door ajar and climbed out, steeling himself for whatever happened next.

There were three hundred yards between life and death; three hundred yards between him and the boy he'd been sent to collect. But this was no valiant act. This was a business transaction, plain and simple. A life for a life. That was Lynch's last offer. Except there was no life to trade for that of the boy's, and now the final minutes of both their lives hung in the balance. Keller had a plan, but if that failed, neither he nor the boy would see the glory of another sunrise. He knew that before he'd agreed to it.

The doors of one of the Navigators eased open and out stepped two figures: one large and dressed all in black, the face hidden beneath a watch cap. The second was much smaller, led by the shoulders by the first figure, their shadows thrown across the blacktop as they stood before the Navigator's headlights.

From this distance, he could only just make out the scared and hollowed face of the boy as his captor lifted the black sack from his head. He stood in the center of the road. The seconds turned to minutes, and behind him came the sound of a third vehicle carried downwind as it pulled sideways across the highway. Roadblocks in both directions now.

He drew in a breath, then walked towards the boy, following the center markings on the road. At the entrance to the underpass, he stopped and called out. "Let him go."

Another voice called out from the darkness. "Who are you?"

"I'm here to take the boy."

"Where's Sullivan?"

As the dark figure pulled the boy closer, Quinn lifted a hand to shield his eyes from the headlights of the Navigators beyond. He counted three more men: two drivers and a third man in the second vehicle. Eyes on, waiting in the shadows like silent assassins.

He glanced down at the boy, who was shaking, his small frame nothing but a bag of bones against the heavy form of his captor. "He's coming," he said, an untruth in every sense of the word but just enough to buy them a few precious minutes more. He checked the time on his wristwatch as the hand stroked the hour.

The call would come. Keller wouldn't let him down.

Just a little longer.

———

Jimmy Lynch finished smoking the rest of his cigarette, his courtyard drenched in the electric blue light from the pool, the warm water as still as a millpond. The mornings were when he was most at peace, before the sun came up and before the rest of the world had woken. The time that existed between yesterday and tomorrow. The time of nocturnal beasts much like himself. As the years had passed, the nights had turned more restless, and the call of a bed had all but eluded him, much to the sorrow of his wife.

He stood at the edge of his pool and took a final drag

on his cigarette, the tip burning to ash. As he looked back at the house, his gaze fell upon the image of his wife stood watching him from the French doors, dressed in a pretty white gown that made her legs look like works of art. Carved from the sharpened blade of the finest sculptor.

"Are you coming to bed tonight?" she said.

Nancy was a patient woman, always had been. He placed the end of his cigarette in the jar lid on the table beside him, then walked over to his wife and kissed her. "Night has come and gone, honey."

Nancy rolled her tired eyes, a kittenish smile on her face. "Well, I won't wait much longer."

He ran a hand across her arm. "Keep it warm for me. I'm not far behind."

"I've heard that before."

He turned from her. "I just need to make a call."

She looked at him with narrowed eyes. "Does this have something to do with what I think it does?"

"I was never much good at reading minds, Nancy. You know that. Go back to bed."

She came close to him and put her arms around his shoulders. "Leave it be. It was a lifetime ago," she said as her soft lips touched the side of his neck.

He pulled away and held her head between his hands. "I'm glad they have your level of forbearance."

She raised a brow. "Who?"

He gestured towards the wall behind her, where a framed picture of their two children hung above the lamp-light. "But you knew the man you married."

His wife nodded in grim acceptance. "Tell me why?" she said. "You told me you'd put that behind you."

"I thought I did," he said as he held his wife close to him. "But he made an oath to me, just like I did to you. An oath you cannot break without consequence." He lifted their hands in unison, displaying their marriage bands.

She kissed him again, then headed for the stairs. He watched her go. He loved his wife, but the woman only knew the spoils of war, not war itself. As his beloved helpmate of twenty years, she was always heard, yet her voice held little weight in the real world in which he revolved. He'd never told her that, of course. Years of marriage had taught him when to keep his mouth shut on such matters. But it was the false virtue that was most vexing to him. Nancy was a woman who would proudly take his arm when the occasion called for it. Yet she was a woman who, behind closed doors, lamented the actions of the man who had given her everything and professed that her hands were clean of blood. That was *her* reality. But in the real one, his wife's hands became as dirty as his own the moment she signed on the dotted line.

As he went out by the pool again, he heard his phone ring.

Then came the scream.

A violent cry that stole the silence.

At once, he turned and hurried back inside the house. He followed the sobs from room to room, down the unlit hallways and called out into the dark of his house. "Nancy?"

He found her in the kitchen, eyes fixed on something in the corner; her face as ashen as the gown in which she stood. As he came in, he laid eyes upon the man that watched from the shadows, eyes smoldering. "Patrick?"

"Not anymore."

"So now you remember?"

"I remember well enough."

"Good," he said, the mere sight of the man in his home enough to turn all color red. A silent rage burning inside him. As the figure of the man he once called a brother limped forward into what pale light could be found, he noticed two things: the gun in his hand, and the look of a man with a bloody-minded purpose.

"Let the boy go."

He looked at his wife and reached for her hand in comfort, but was left holding nothing as she pulled it away. He went to the window and looked out: a body sprawled on the driveway, another by the entrance to the house. Both his men were dead on the ground.

"No one's coming for you."

He turned his attention back to the bastard before him who stood like the Angel of Death, ready to do his work. "My wife has nothing to do with this."

"Neither did the boy."

Nancy sobbed but stayed silent.

"What's the plan here, Patrick?" he said.

"I already told you. Let the boy go and I leave. I give you my word."

"Just like that?"

"Just like that."

"Do what he says, Jimmy!" His wife was shaking now as the tears came flowing.

That was when he heard a third voice. The voice of his daughter as she came in, calling out for her father as she reached for the light switch on the wall, the smaller shape of her brother by her side.

"Dad?"

Nancy drew in a horrified breath at the sight of her children and rushed to their side. "Please, let us leave..." she said.

Cold eyes returned the desperate plea as the pistol took aim. "Nobody leaves until you make that call."

"Okay," he said, the stricken faces of his family looking at him, pleading. "I'll make the call. But this is between you and me alone. Let them go." He edged his way round the center island as Nancy threw her arms around their children and pulled them close.

"I don't think you're in a position to be making demands," the bastard said. "But what you do have is a choice, and that is more than you gave me."

He fixed Sullivan to the wall with a stare as he reached a hand into his pocket, rage pulsing behind his gritted teeth. He pulled out his cell, punched in a number, feigned the call, then looked up again. "Reception dropped. It's better in the entrance hall."

Sullivan nodded, fell for the ruse.

"Stay there," he said, kissing his son and daughter once each on the forehead as he went by.

The bastard followed him back into the unlit entrance hall, one eye on him, the other on his family. He looked up towards the top of the dresser in the hallway where he kept his piece. A Colt 1911, hidden from view but within reach. A full clip in the chamber, cocked and locked. He only needed a second to even the score, and there was no way this sonofabitch was walking out of here on two legs. Not again.

Sullivan pointed his pistol. "Get on with it."

He positioned himself in front of the dresser and dialed the number. For real this time. It rang three times. "Let him go," he said.

A rough voice responded in kind. "Sir?"

"Let the boy go." He kept the phone pressed to his ear and waited for what felt like the longest moment of his life.

No less than a minute had passed when he heard Sullivan's phone go off. The call to tell him the boy was safe. The call he had been waiting for. The moment of distraction.

As Sullivan lifted the phone, he stretched an arm for the 1911 atop the dresser. The faces of his wife and children looked on in abject horror as he clawed for the pistol. The black steel of the barrel came down across his body and settled somewhere on Sullivan's body, who barely had time to blink.

The first round hit the drywall as Sullivan moved, the phone tumbling from his grip. The second ended up somewhere in the doorjamb as he tried to focus his aim.

The bastard raised his gun to meet him.

Lynch saw the muzzle flash and nothing else. He was dead before he hit the floor.

———

Quinn waited in the center of the road as the boy crossed the hundred yards to meet him, his small face like that of any terrified and confused ten-year-old unmasked in darkness and told to walk towards another unknown.

"Who are you?" the boy said as he lifted his head against the dawning light.

"Jacob sent me," he said.

"To get me?"

"Yes."

"Is he your friend?"

"I suppose he is."

"He's my friend, too."

"Then I guess that makes us friends as well."

The boy looked back over his shoulder. The men who had brought him here still lingering at the edge of the tunnel.

He looked the boy up and down. "Are you hurt?"

The boy shook his head. "I'm okay."

"Wait in the car," he said, his eyes fixed dead ahead at Lynch's men stood beside their vehicles and clad in black like headsman in waiting. Semi-automatics cradled in their arms.

"Where are you going?"

"I'm right behind you," he said to the boy. "Now go."

When the boy was in the car, he pulled his cellphone and made the call to Jacob. All that remained to be done was to get the hell out of the city and the boy some place far from here.

The phone rang without an answer. In the distance, he saw the men moving in the tunnel again, their shoulders hunched as they took aim with their rifles. He turned as he heard the report of the first shot. Another figure had quit the vehicle that was blocking the highway behind, now advancing on his rear.

Glass shattered on his leg as the second round struck the headlight on the Crown Vic. He squatted on his haunches and crawled towards the rear of the Crown Vic. Soon the break of day was filled with the burst of gunfire as a hail of rounds ricocheted off the hood of the car, punching holes in the side panels.

He popped the trunk and reached in for the AR15 laid flat in its case. Two magazines beside it. He loaded a clip and took up the weapon, stock to his shoulder, his finger finding the trigger. He returned with shots of his own, firing wildly at the black masses approaching until the magazine was empty and he was dry firing. One figure dropped to the blacktop, unmoving. "Head down!" he said, spotting the boy frozen in the passenger seat when he turned again, his face the color of alabaster behind the windshield. "Get your head down!"

The lifting shadows lit up in a blaze of muzzle flash. Another body dropped somewhere in the distance, then he felt his own knee give way beneath him. The round had entered just to the right of his navel. His insides burned like hell. Only adrenaline to numb the pain as he struggled to his feet again.

He sighted the figure approaching from his rear, crisscrossing the highway in the darkness as he dumped three rounds. The gunman stumbled to the side of the road, then slumped from view in the tall grass like a slain animal.

He turned once more, acting on instinct. In the light of the tunnel, he watched as the last gunman retreated towards the waiting Navigator, climbed in, and threw it into reverse. As he limped forward, he opened fire on the fading Navigator until its tail lights were lost to the darkness beyond.

The cold air steadied him and the taste of blood in his mouth brought him back to the moment. Finally, the boy's head rose into view behind the windshield, eyes as wide as nickels. He limped towards the Crown Vic, one hand pressed hard to his abdomen as he laid the AR15 on the back seat, panting like a dog. "You hit?"

The boy checked himself. Not a visible scratch on him. "I don't think so."

Silence replaced the sound of gunfire. Then his cellphone rang again. "What the fuck happened?" he said, lifting the phone to his ear.

Keller was on the other end and short of breath. "Nevermind," Jacob said. "Do you have him?"

"The boy's safe. You?"

"I'm fine."

"Lynch?"

"Not so fine."

He walked round to the driver's side of the Crown Vic and got in. "I'm on my way."

Keller paused. "You don't sound good."

"Don't feel it either." He talked through the pain, the bottom of his shirt soaked with blood. He kept a palm pressed to his stomach, trying to keep his guts from spilling out onto the leather seats. He'd seen a liver shot before and knew his chances of seeing out this morning were slim to none.

A knowing silence filled the seconds.

"How long do you have?" Keller said.

"How long do you need?"

Another pause. "There's a strip mall in Andorra. Can you make it?"

He looked at the boy sat small in the seat beside him. "I'll be there."

———

"Are you going to die?" the boy asked.

Quinn eyed the road, one hand on the wheel as he wiped the cold sweat from his face. He felt a chill run over him and his eyes grow heavier with each mile that passed, his body all but quitting on him. "What do you know about it?"

"I've seen people die."

"Is that a fact?"

"Yes, sir."

He rolled down the window to let the air in. Anything to keep him awake a little longer. Anything to keep him alive longer than that.

"I'll pray for you," the boy said.

"Better do it quick, son. God's on a clock and I'm all out of coins." He looked down to see the boy's hand on top of his. "You remind me of my daughter."

The boy looked at him. "What's her name?"

The presentness of the question took him aback. "Chloe," he said, a whisper now. "Her name is Chloe."

The boy closed his eyes and pressed his palms together in a wordless prayer.

Time seemed to stop. The highway was empty in both directions, and the fading stars seemed to hang in the dawning sky like paper lanterns, guiding him to whatever waited in the great beyond.

His shallow breaths had all but ceased when he wheeled the Crown Vic into the vacant parking lot, and whatever life he had left in him was departing with each slowing beat of his heart.

The shape of a man appeared at his window as the car slowed to a dead stop, and his eyes met those of Jacob Keller's for the last time.

"Can you get out?" Keller said.

"I ain't going nowhere," he replied.

"Can I do anything for you?"

He winced as he turned in his seat, every word a struggle. "Too late for that."

Keller nodded as the boy quit the car to join him, their faces grim in the pre-dawn light, but a look of gratitude in their eyes.

"Be gone," he said.

Keller reached in with a hand and placed it on his shoulder in silent thanks. When he glanced up a final time, they were gone, and he saw nothing but the fading stars again. He felt the cold against his face and the wind in his hair and the weight of his eyes as he willed them open, just one last time, to see the world again. As he lied back in the seat, he reached a hand into his pocket for his phone and searched for the only number he could think of. It rang as he lifted the phone to his ear.

"Hey, this is Chloe. I can't find my phone right now, so I'll call you back. Unless it's my dad, in which case, I'm still looking for it. Leave a message if you want."

His last thought was of his daughter, waiting for him at the port of the promised land. For whatever lied on the other side of this dark night was nothing but his quiet, final exit.

Chapter 33

The days turned to nights, and the nights to days again, yet no one came for them. Not yet. But they would be looking, of that he was certain. He and the boy spent the first three nights in a motel room on the edge of the city. A place to lie low. A place to buy them some time. He shaved off his beard and hair until there was nothing left, and dyed the boys black to hide the blond. They left on the fourth night and hitched a ride west, which brought them to an old farmstead where they were greeted by an old man with more teeth than brains, and of those that he'd salvaged had turned black from rot.

The old man bled him for every cent, but he had little option as he walked him round the vehicle, kicking the tires with his boot. It was cash on collection, no questions asked. Ten minutes later, he and the boy left in a '76 Dodge Street Van the color of rusted vomit. She was no head turner, but she slept two in the back and came with some dusty blankets for the frosty nights ahead. This wouldn't be their life forever, he'd make sure of it. But it would be their home for now and would make do.

They kept their heads down and their faces hidden, and three more days passed before they finally made the journey back to the city. He had to see her face just one last time, to know she was still alive.

"Wait here," he said as they pulled up outside Jefferson Memorial.

"What's here?" the boy said.

He sighed and shook his head. "A bad conscience."

The boy narrowed his eyes. "I don't understand what that means."

"Good. I hope you never have to find out." He climbed out of the Dodge and turned back to the boy. "Keep the doors locked. I won't be long."

He checked his shoulder as he walked towards the entrance to the hospital and pulled his ball cap low, then reached into his coat pocket and withdrew the necklace that he had carried with him every night since he had left her here without so much as a soul who knew her name. He searched three wards before he sighted her through the window of a single-bed room; her face swollen and discolored, but never enough to steal her beauty.

Amanda was sitting up in the bed and talking with a man in a chair next to her, who held her hand and bowed his head as though in prayer. At first he didn't recognize the man, but when he lifted his chin and wiped his eyes, he looked upon the face of her father, sat at his daughter's bedside with nothing else but a look of wholehearted love.

He stood and watched them for a moment and let the wave of relief pass over him. She was alive. That was the only thing that mattered. But this was not the time or the place for a reunion. Maybe there never would be.

As he turned to leave, the nurse behind him raised a smile as she approached the door to Amanda's room, donning her surgical gloves.

"Are you family?" the nurse said.

"No," he said. "A friend."

"She's not long woken up. Do you want me to let her know you're here?"

"No," he said, then handed the nurse the necklace, "but could you give her this?"

The nurse nodded as she took the necklace from him. "Of course."

And with that, he left.

———

"Is it good again?" the boy asked as he climbed back into the van and sat at the wheel.

"Is what good?"

"Whatever you said was here earlier. Is it good again?"

"My conscience?" he said, giving thought to it. "Yeah, I guess it is." He managed a smile as the boy turned to him with all the unworldly innocence that only a child possessed. And in that moment, he knew what he had to do. He would do right by the boy. They'd head west, into the desert where he'd heard of places where no one would ask questions. Where the lost souls of the world gathered in their masses. He would find the boy somewhere safe where they could be together. Somewhere where his son would never have to learn of the sins of his father.

So they drove on, into the night, into whatever new tomorrow that awaited them.

Epilogue

Erin Moss walked down the long white corridor, sipping her coffee as she approached the security desk with her keycard and let herself through. The night warden tipped his head in greeting as she went through the locked door, then returned to the book he was reading. As she looked further down the corridor, she noticed Fraser coming towards her at a clip. A look of puerile excitement on his face.

"He's awake," he said.

"Since when?"

"Just this minute."

She followed Fraser towards the room at the far end and took a breath to steady herself as she entered.

It was his eyes she noticed first: distant, cold. Just like all of them when they awoke, as if trying to make sense between the fog of their new reality.

His name was David Ayres, at least that was the name they had given him.

Ayres was lying flat on the bed, his arm hooked up to an IV line. He rolled his head to one side and caught her gaze as she came forward, eyes narrowing in the harsh light. And yet, in his narcotized state, she couldn't tell if he was looking *at* her or just right through her.

Fraser squatted beside him. "Mr. Ayres? My name is Dr. Fraser."

The man tried to speak, but no words followed.

"You were in an accident," Fraser said, assuming the usual narrative.

It seemed so weird to her now, stood here like this, listening to the line she had rehearsed herself so many times before.

His name had been Eugene Garett before. Convicted child molester and sentenced as such. She'd read the report. The perfect candidate. He looked the same, but everything else about him seemed different. Everything else about him *was* different. That was the purpose of the program.

Finally, he managed a whisper. "What kind of accident?"

"A car accident," she said. It came out without a thought, and she just stood and watched, looking down at the husk of the man that she had helped create.

Fraser stepped between them as the man's eyes searched for hers. "Do you know where you are?"

The man shook his head. He did not.

"Can you tell me your name?" Fraser asked, leaning closer now.

She could see Ayres trying to reach for it, search for it. But nothing came.

"My head hurts," the man said, lifting a hand towards his temple.

She carried on watching as Ayres searched for the voices that spoke to him, trying to piece together whatever fragments of torn memories that remained to make sense of it all. She reached a hand to touch his and held it tightly as she kneeled beside his bed and asked him, "Can you tell me the last thing you remember?"

A Note from the Author

Thanks for choosing **The Good Citizen**. I hope you enjoyed it.

As a reader, I know how hard it can be to take a chance on a new book. As a writer, I know how hard it is to put something out there which you feel is worthy of someone's time and attention.

If you liked this book, I'd be very grateful if you could spare a few moments of your time letting me know by **leaving an honest review** from the store you purchased it from. Reviews go a long way in helping me continue writing what you enjoy, and helping books reach the right readers.

Thank you,

Marc Ross

About the Author

Before becoming a writer, Marc Ross worked in a maximum security prison, law enforcement, and, more recently, practiced in law. *The Good Citizen* is his debut novel.